0.00
4/10
W

D0811130

COLEG LLANDRILLO CYMRU
CANOLFAN ADNODDAU LLYFRGELL
LIBRARY RESOURCE CENTRE
FFON/TEL 01492 54234?

CHESTERFIELD
LIBRARY
CAN~ ODDA~ ~LL

general   4/10
100560   LRC   Fic HAY

THE
MATEWIX

THE
MATEWIX

CHARLIE HAMILTON JAMES

HarperCollins*Entertainment*
An Imprint of HarperCollinsPublishers

This novel is entirely a work of fiction. The names,
characters and incidents portrayed in it are the work of the
author's imagination. Any resemblance to actual persons,
living or dead, events or localities is entirely coincidental.

HarperCollins*Entertainment*
An Imprint of HarperCollins*Publishers*
77–85 Fulham Palace Road,
Hammersmith, London W6 8JB

www.harpercollins.co.uk

Published by HarperCollins*Entertainment* 2003
3 5 7 9 8 6 4

Copyright © Charlie Hamilton James 2003

The Author asserts the moral right to
be identified as the author of this work

A catalogue record for this book
is available from the British Library

ISBN 0 00 717690 2

Set in Sabon
Printed and bound in Great Britain by Clays Lts, St Ives plc

All rights reserved. No part of this publication may be
reproduced, stored in a retrieval system, or transmitted,
in any form or by any means, electronic, mechanical,
photocopying, recording or otherwise, without the prior
permission of the publishers.

This book is sold subject to the condition that it shall not,
by way of trade or otherwise, be lent, re-sold, hired out or
otherwise circulated without the publisher's prior consent
in any form of binding or cover other than that in which it
is published and without a similar condition including this
condition being imposed on the subsequent purchaser.

THE
MATEWIX

Based on a film by the
NOAMCHOMSKY BROTHERS

In *The Matewix* our hero, Newo, has a rather bad speech impediment which gets him into all sorts of twuble in a world that's not quite what it seems.

'If you take the red pill, Newo, there is no going back. You will leave the Matewix and enter a world more real to you than you can possibly imagine.

But, Newo, if you take the blue pill you will sustain an erection for up to twelve years ... The question is, Newo, what's it to be? The red pill or the blue pill?'

'I'll take both,' replied Newo, and chucked them both down his throat.

CHAPTER ONE

WAY OF THE GEEK

'I'm putting it into your hard drive now, Titty,' said Siphon.

'Are you floppy?' asked Titty as she banged away on the keyboard.

'Not any more,' replied Siphon with a hint of excitement in his voice. 'I'm fully loaded. What's the key code?'

'Amorphous wouldn't tell me,' replied Titty. 'He just strapped it on while I was sleeping.'

Siphon raised an eyebrow, put the tape into his ZX81 and pressed play on the tape recorder. 'You think he is the Number Two, don't you?'

Titty said nothing. She just squirmed a little and adjusted the PVC around her gusset. 'Amorphous does ... and I trust Amorphous.'

'i'm in!' shouted Siphon.

'Go, go, go!' Titty started bouncing up and down frantically and moaning, 'He is the Number Two, he is the Number Two!'

'Not now, Titty!'

Titty turned frantically to Siphon. 'Have I got a clean line?' she asked. 'Is it bugged? It shouldn't be. I went to the clinic last week.'

'I don't know. I can't tell till I'm out … We've got to get out.'

The tapes jammed. 'Pull out, pull out!'

Titty leaped off her keyboard and went for the door. It burst open and Jet Set Willy flew in, all guns blazing.

'Get out, Titty!' shouted Siphon. 'Get out!'

Titty rolled across the floor, ran across the ceiling and planted one square into Willy's nuts.

'There's one on Seventh and Maine. You can make it,' shouted Siphon as she shot out the door, leaving the poor computer hero bent foetal, clasping his gooseberries.

She raced down the green corridor and leaped out

of a first-floor window, crashing to the ground three and a half feet below. She jumped to her feet and shot off, not even apologizing to the woman whose Yorkshire Terrier had died softening her landing. She rounded a corner or two and burst through a green door into another green corridor. 'Where now, Operator?' she shouted down her phone.

'The number you have dialled has not been recognized,' replied a voice.

She stopped and frantically redialled, sweat dripping from her forehead and running down her neck into her pert bosom. 'Come on, Siphon!' she snarled at the phone. 'Operator!' she shouted as the phone was answered.

'Welcome to the *Knobachaneza*,' came the voice. 'Please listen carefully to the following options. If you are in the Matewix and unable to find a suitable place for lunch and/or light refreshment, please press 1.' Titty turned frantically to look around for Agent Provocateurs. 'If you are in the Matewix and need a number two, please press 2.'

She threw the phone down and ran. She ran and

ran until the sweat from her forehead had breached her panties and started chafing her inner thigh.

'Come on, Titty,' said Amorphous, who had come over to Siphon and was watching the drama from the main deck of the *Knobachaneza*. 'Come on! Get yourself out of there.'

Titty heard the phone and burst through the green door on her left. 'Bingo!' she shouted and picked it up. She was out.

Newo sat slumped over his Atari ST. His room was a mess of half-eaten pizzas and porno mags. On his stereo wailed his favourite band, Westlife, and on his walls hung torn and stained pictures of Steps and Maurice Gibb.

His computer flashed in front of him, lighting his spotty face and buzzing a little. Words suddenly started scrolling across the screen. '*Stop wanking, Newo,*' was the first line. Then, '*We need to meat.*'

Newo pulled his eyes open and lifted his head. He gazed in confusion at the monitor. '*Don't you mean "meet"?*' he typed back.

'No, *meat*,' came the reply.

Newo raised his eyebrows and smiled. '*Well hello there, babe*,' he typed.

'*There's no time for foreplay, Newo*,' came the reply. '*Follow the Welsh rarebit*.'

A knock bounced off the door. Newo brushed a couple of *Men Only*s, a *Razzle*, two copies of *Skinny and Wriggly*, a *Playboy*, another three *Razzle*s and a *Readers' Wives Special* off his lap and went for the door. He was nervous. Maybe it was the cops, the Feds, the CIA, the environmental health, his mum. He stuck an eye up to the spy hole and looked. 'Who is it?' he asked.

'Rupert,' came the reply.

'You got the bwead, Wupert?' asked Newo as he opened the door.

'Yes, I have it,' replied Rupert.

Standing in the dark green hallway were five people: a skinny bloke in his late teens clutching a loaf of thick cut Kingsmill, a goofy Welsh girl called Gwynedd who wore a knitted T-shirt and a Shakin' Stevens sweatband, a nun in her late fifties who harboured fantasies of butch lesbianism, a Goth girl who had no charisma or obvious attractive qualities, and her boyfriend who looked the same but smelled of Vicks and Duraglit.

'You got the dough?' asked the skinny guy with the loaf.

'Wait wight thewe while I wun and get it,' said Newo. He shut the door and returned a couple of seconds later with a bag of half-risen dough.

'Are you coomin oot tonight, intit?' asked the Welsh girl, as Newo and the skinny bloke exchanged yeast-based products.

'Where are you going?' asked Newo.

The girl smiled at him seductively. 'Ronnie's.'

'Wonnie's, eh?' replied Newo.

'Ronnie the Red Rabbit's Right Rollocking Rabble-rousing Rabid Ragga Rave.'

Newo swallowed slightly and nodded. 'Wonnie's,' he said again. 'I think I'll stay in tonight and wead.'

The girl tried not to laugh, and winked at him. 'You don't want to come to the Ragga Rave?' she asked one more time.

Then Newo saw it, stuck to her back just above her bra strap – a soggy old piece of cheese on toast. '*Follow the Welsh rarebit,*' Newo recalled. He gazed at the girl a little, and she winked at him again. 'I'll come,' he declared. 'Wait thewe while I get my waincoat.'

Ronnie's was packed. It was loud and sweaty and the crowd were all slam dancing in the mosh pit to Ronan Keating. Newo forced his way through the thick crowd, trying to snatch morsels of cheese off the Welsh rarebit that was still stuck to Gwynedd's back. Then suddenly she was gone and Newo found himself alone, chewing on a piece of Wensleydale. A woman came up to him and touched him on the shoulder. He span round to meet her eyes.

'Hello, Newo,' she said.

Newo looked at her suspiciously. 'How do you know my handle?' he asked.

'I know everything about you,' replied the woman. 'I know what toilet paper you use, I know how big your overdraft is, I know how many times you piss a day, how you keep your copies of *Razzle* in date order, how many times you masturbate a day and how many packets of Bachelor's Tummy Wipes you get through a week.' She paused to take a breath. 'How big your ...'

'Stop!' begged Newo. 'That's pwobably enough. Who are you?'

The woman looked hard into his eyes. 'I'm Titty,' she replied.

Newo looked surprised. 'What, *the* Titty?'

'Yes, *the* Titty,' replied Titty.

'Titty Tyson, the bweast boxing bitch of Bawwow-in-Fuwness?' asked Newo.

'No!' replied Titty, slightly horrified. 'Just *the* Titty.'

Newo shrugged.

'They're watching you, Newo.'

Concern crept into Newo's expression. 'Who awe?' he asked.

'The Agent Provocateurs,' replied Titty.

Newo shrank back a little.

'You know it's out there, don't you, Newo? You know there's something out there.'

Newo nodded slightly.

'Amorphous wants to meat you, Newo.'

Newo looked slightly shocked. 'Do you mean "meet"?' he asked.

'Sorry, yes,' replied Titty.

Newo sighed with relief and relaxed his buttocks.

'He will contact you. He will explain ...' Titty backed off slightly and looked hard into Newo's eyes. 'He will show you the Matewix, Newo.'

Newo's expression brightened a notch. 'What is the Matewix?' he asked with wide eyes.

Titty backed off even more. 'Amorphous will explain all, Newo. You are the Number Two!'

And she was gone. Newo stood stunned, looking across the dancers and strobes wondering why him – why was he the 'Number Two'?

Newo was draining the fat off the fries and whistling 'Lady in Red' by Chris de Burgh. He'd got a bollocking for being late for work again and was trying to make up for it by being extra careful and not pissing in the chips. Flipping burgers in Burglar

King was not his ideal career, but all that was about to change.

'Mr Sanderson?' came a voice from the counter.

Newo looked over. 'Yes,' he replied.

'I have a package for you, Mr Sanderson.'

Newo went over to the counter, signed for the package and took it over to the burger freezer to open it. Inside was a mobile phone. He picked it up and looked at it, wondering why he'd been sent a mobile phone. It rang. Newo almost dropped it, he was so shocked. He fumbled with it, trying to find out how to answer it.

'Hello, Newo,' came the voice when he finally did.

'Who is this?' he asked.

'The question is not "Who is this?", Newo, the question is "Why is this?"'

Newo held the phone out from his ear and looked at it strangely. 'No, the question is "Who is this?"'

'The question is "When is this?"' the voice said.

'Twat!' shouted Newo and hung up. The phone rang again.

'Hello, Newo,' came the voice again.

'Who is this?' asked Newo.

'The question is not "Who ..." It's Amorphous,' said the voice. 'You've been expecting me, haven't you, Newo? You've been waiting.'

Newo shook his head. 'No, not weally,' he replied.

'They're coming for you, Newo.'

'Who are?' asked Newo.

'The Agent Provocateurs,' replied Amorphous.

'Whewe awe they?' asked Newo. He looked about but couldn't see anything.

'They're on till three, Newo.'

Newo peered round the bun griller and caught sight of three men wearing sunglasses, and a load of cops. They saw him and leaped the counter, knocking all the milk shake straws off as they went.

'What do I do?' begged Newo down the phone.

'The blue door on your left, Newo. Go through it.'

Newo looked over at the door. 'It's the ladies!' he whispered.

'Do it!' came the reply.

He dashed for the door and charged through it.

'Now get into a cubicle and wait.'

17

Newo tried the closest cubicle, but it was locked. 'Sowwy!' he shouted and shot into the next one.

The Agent Provocateurs burst in and looked under the doors. Newo pulled his feet up onto the seat and froze.

'There's a small window above the sink, Newo. It is open. You must leap through it when I tell you.'

Newo nodded.

The Agent Provocateurs and the cops filed out of the ladies. 'Now!' shouted Amorphous.

Newo burst out of the cubicle and went for the window. Suddenly fear shot through him as he hung out of the window over a six-foot abyss. 'I can't do it,' he whispered frantically down the phone.

'You have a choice, Newo,' said Amorphous 'You make the jump and leave with me, or you stay and leave with them.'

Newo swayed, dizzied by the height. 'I have a wecuwwing gwoin stwain,' he hissed. 'If I jump I'll surely stwain it again.' He shook his head angrily at the chasm below him, and gave up.

* * *

'Mr Sanderson,' said Agent Smiff as he stared hard at Newo across the desk. 'My colleagues, Cline and Beacham, have … been watching you … hmmm.'

Newo looked at Smiff, Cline and Beacham; they stared back at him. He gazed about the green, undecorated cell and tried to compose himself.

'Mr Sanderson … hmm … You have been party to …' Smiff opened a large file and began to thumb through it '… just about every bread-based crime there is a law for, haven't you, Mr Sanderson?'

Newo said nothing.

Smiff hung on the silence for a while. 'I'll be straight with you, Mr Sanderson. You have been contacted by a man … I think you know who I am talking about … hmm, yes … He is a terrorist, probably the most wanted man in the whole of Wales. We need you, Mr Sanderson … We need you to help us contact him.'

Newo said nothing.

'Now, Mr Sanderson, you have two options. You help us and we'll … well, let's say we'll wipe the stain clean. Or, Mr Sanderson, you continue to deal in bread-based products and occasionally hack computers … and I get to shag your sister.'

Newo looked up, surprised. 'I don't have a sister,' he protested.

'Hmm …' Smiff sat back in his chair. 'You do, Mr Sanderson, you do.'

Newo looked confused.

'She's called Pamela,' explained Smiff. 'Pamela Sanderson.'

'No!' shouted Newo. 'She's not my sister!'

Smiff grinned like a shit-eater. 'Queen of the Handy Shandy … hmm … I believe, Mr Sanderson, that she has a nice pair of bazookas … hmm … top bollocks … I believe one could hang a wet duffel coat off them, Mr Sanderson.'

'She's not my sister,' protested Newo again.

'She is, Mr Sanderson, she is. You share a father, Mr Sanderson. I have the reports.' Smiff shoved a couple of DNA print-outs over to Newo and sat back in his chair.

'She can't be!' Newo looked about, horrified 'But I … but I … I tossed …'

'Yes, Mr Sanderson, you did.'

Newo shot glances around the room, looking for an escape, a clue to why he was there, anything.

'It's useless, Mr Sanderson. There is no way out. This facility … hmm … is in the heart of the Welsh valleys. If you did manage to escape you would be killed and eaten within hours. By the locals, Mr Sanderson … hmm.'

Newo chewed a fingernail and shook slightly.

'This terrorist … Amorphous, I believe his name is … Yes … He has contacted you, Mr Sanderson, and you are going to help us contact him.'

Newo shook his head and tried to force a defiant grin, but he just looked like a frightened Brownie.

'What do you say, Mr Sanderson?'

Newo looked hard at the wall and then at Cline and back to Beacham. 'I tell you what I am going to do,' he said, sitting back in his chair. 'I'm going to show you this.' He stick two fingers up at Smiff. 'And you're going to give me my phone call.'

Smiff grinned and leaned towards Newo. 'What use is a phone call, Mr Sanderson, if you don't have 10p?'

Newo looked terrified. He fell backwards out of his chair, patting his pockets frantically, tugging at his wallet.

'It's no use,' shouted Smiff. 'You only have a £2 coin, Mr Sanderson, and the phone doesn't take anything bigger than 50p.'

'NOOOO!!!" shouted Newo as he emptied his purse full of coppers and £2 coins out on the floor. Suddenly Cline and Beacham were on him. They grappled with his arm and forced him over the desk.

'So be it, Mr Sanderson,' said Smiff as he strolled round the desk. Cline ripped down Newo's trousers. 'It's whelk time!' Smiff pulled a whelk from his pocket. It had an ominous-looking tracking device attached to its shell. Beacham ripped down Newo's burgundy Y-fronts and kicked his legs apart. 'They say that all living creatures need sunlight to survive, Mr Sanderson ... hmm ... I think perhaps this whelk here may prove them wrong.'

'NNNNOOOO!!!!!'

CHAPTER TWO

GEEK MYTHOLOGY

'Why should I trust you?' asked Newo.

Titty cast around for an answer.

'Because if you don't you'll have a whelk stuck up your arse,' interrupted Stitch.

'That's right,' continued Titty. 'A whelk up your arse.'

Titty pulled out one of those special forks the French use for pulling snails out of their shells, and Newo drew back in fear.

'Don't you have anything more sophisticated than that? A vacuum cleaner type thing? A big sywinge, pewhaps? Anything but the Fwench fork!'

Titty smiled calmly. 'The French have been using these for hundreds of years to extract snails from their shells and put them into their mouths, Newo. I don't see your arse is much different to a Frenchman's mouth, now is it?'

Newo shook his head but remained terrified.

Siphon swung the Mini Metro round another tight corner and the passengers in the back all fell together.

'Couldn't we at least wait until we've stopped moving?' asked Newo.

Titty shook her head and closed in. Newo threw his legs in the air and screamed, 'NNNNOOOO!!!!!'

It was pissing with rain when they arrived at the Holiday Inn. They rushed through the foyer and into the lift. Newo was limping severely and Titty had to hurry him. They got out on the third floor and made their way down a green corridor until they got to Room 303. They knocked and entered. Inside there was a man: Amorphous. He stood with his back to Newo and Titty, looking out the window at the rain.

'Hello, Newo,' said Amorphous. He turned round. He was tall and dark and wore dark sunglasses. He scouted about the room with his eyes as if looking for something.

'We're over here, Amorphous,' said Titty.

Amorphous found them. 'It's dark in here,' he said. 'I think it's these sunglasses,' he continued, fiddling with the rim. 'We have finally found you, Newo.'

Newo stepped forward. 'It is a gweat honour to meet you, Amowphous,' he said, putting out a hand. Amorphous felt about a bit until he found the hand and shook it.

'The pleasure, my dear boy, is all mine.' He smiled. Newo smiled and nodded and tried to withdraw his hand, but Amorphous kept hold of it. 'I have been looking for you, Newo. I have been looking for you for a very long time … To be or not to be, Newo? That is the question.'

Newo nodded. 'Is it?'

'The question is not "To be or not to be?", Newo. The question is "*When* to be", not "Not to be or to be".'

'Weally,' replied Newo, slightly perplexed.

Amorphous broke his hand grip and went for a masterly stroll about the room. 'Do you know *why* you are here, Newo?'

'Well ...'

'The question is not "Do you know why you're here?" Newo; the question is "*When* are you here?"'

Newo shrugged.

Amorphous banged his head on the fake plastic chandelier and grabbed his temple in pain. 'Damned glasses,' he cursed. 'I expect you feel like Ratty from *Wind in the Willows*, don't you, Newo? Going out for a spin in Toad's car ... Racing through the streets of middle England, never sure where you are going to go or where it's going to end. Like being in a dream world.'

Newo nodded.

'Have you ever had a wet dream that you were sure was real, Newo? A wet dream that you couldn't wake from?'

Newo nodded. 'Isn't that evewy man's dweam?' he asked.

'But you always wake up, don't you, Newo? Just as it's all starting to happen ... As if someone somewhere is pulling a plug. It's like your mum bringing in a cup of tea at the worst moment, isn't it,

Newo? Then waking up to find that she's not there and she never was ... It's like the Matewix, Newo ... And when you wake up from it naked and covered in slime you will understand. Does anyone here know what the Matewix is?' he asked, moving back towards Newo.

Newo put his hand up; so did Titty.

'Newo,' said Amorphous. 'Yes ... do you know what the Matewix is?'

'Is it a specially designed filter unit for pwocessing and collecting bwoad beans?'

Amorphous shook his head.

'Is it a form of scweensaver that continuously scwolls illegible numbers and digits in an appawently totally wandom way, but which, to the all-knowing mind, makes up a complex and deceitful weality in the minds of a species that has been forced into slavewy by the mistakes of its own awwogant pweoccupations?'

Amorphous strolled a bit and thought. 'Possibly ... The Matewix is all around you, Newo. It is the chair you are – please sit down ...' Newo did ...'– sitting on, the air you breathe, the absurd speech impediment you have, and Titty's fantastic rack ... Although she often takes that back to the mother ship with her ... but that is not the question; the question is not "What is the Matewix?" The question is "What is the question?", Newo. I can show you the question, but you have to answer it.'

Newo looked confused. 'What is it then?' he begged.

'The Matewix?' asked Amorphous.

'No, the question,' replied Newo.

'The question, Newo, is "What is the Matewix?"'

Newo looked more confused. Amorphous banged his head on the chandelier again. 'Look, *whatever*, here are two pills, Newo. A red pill and a blue pill. The red pill will open up a world to you more real than you can possibly imagine; a world where green corridors and ropey philosophical quotations go hand in hand; a world where Toad will show you how fast his car really can go. And the blue pill. The blue pill, Newo. The blue pill will give you an erection that you will sustain for up to twelve years.'

Newo's eyes lit up a little. 'The question is, Newo, what's it to be? The red pill or the blue pill?'

'I'll take both,' replied Newo and chucked them both down his throat.

'Would you like a cup of tea?' asked Stitch. Newo looked at her, blurry eyed, and gurgled a bit. 'I'll put the kettle on, shall I? Yes, I will, I will.' She rubbed her hands together in a motherly way. 'Would anyone else like a cup of tea? Titty? Amorphous? Siphon? No? Shrew? Epoch?' No one answered, and the unattractive blonde girl went off to make one for herself and Newo.

'He's wired,' suggested Epoch to Amorphous. 'He's so wired he's dribbling on his leg. Shall we wheel him through now?'

'Whatever will be, will be,' said Amorphous.

'I'll take that as a yes, then, shall I?' replied Epoch.

'Yes is the answer and the answer is none less than yes,' replied Amorphous. He turned and walked back over to the window. 'Titty,' he asked, 'Titty, have you done your room?'

Titty shrunk back a little. 'Er, no, Amorphous. No, I haven't had time; I've been in and out of the Matewix like a yo-yo of late and, well, I've been getting in knackered every night and all I can think of doing when I get in is peeling off my PVC catsuit, taking off my hot wet bra and panties and getting into bed.'

'Hmm ...' said Amorphous. 'To sleep! Perchance to dream!'

Shrew came running in. 'He's ready. The trace is ready ... It's all ready.'

Amorphous and Titty followed Shrew into an adjoining bedroom where Newo was sitting in a chair surrounded by typewriters, fax machines, a couple of ZX81s, a tape recorder, a BBC B and an Acorn Computer. He had wires running all over him, some in his mouth, some in his ears and a couple up each nostril.

'Are you sure this is going to work?' asked Titty. 'I have to say it looks a little dated. What's wrong with using modern computers? Why all the ancient stuff?'

Epoch grinned and took Titty by the hand. 'Look,

Titty,' he explained. 'It's all wired up back here to a 4-litre Lister diesel engine. That kit rocks shit, man!'

Titty looked shocked as Epoch pulled the curtain back to reveal the hulking beast, spluttering heavily on the soiled red diesel Siphon had siphoned out of a tractor a few days before. 'That's incredible,' she remarked.

'We got him!' shouted Shrew. Newo started thrashing and jerking violently. The others ran over to see what was going on. 'We got him! We got him!' shouted Shrew again.

'Where is he?' queried Amorphous.

Shrew cast his eyes across the television screens that the computers were wired into. 'Sssswwwiindon ... Swindon.'

Newo jerked into life. He sat bolt upright, gasping and terrified. He looked about; fear rode his eyes. He was bright orange, covered head to foot in baked beans and alphabet spaghetti. The hair on his head was thick and matted and went all the way down his back. His beard was almost as long, and he had mutton chops that stuck out almost a foot, all matted with baked beans, bits of sausage, fried eggs and bacon rind. He picked a half-eaten Ferrero Rocher off his nose and groaned in disgust. He looked about. He was in a slop bucket full of food and wires. They went into him in various places – the back of his head, his back, his arms, his legs, and another place, and about them sloshed beans and food of all colours and varieties. There were even occasional bits of packaging among the slosh.

Newo skimmed the tomato bean sauce off his arms and leaned forward to see what lay around him. Horror filled his face. Beyond him, for as far as he could see, were hundreds and hundreds of identical slop buckets filled with bearded men and the occasional bearded woman. Above him and below him he looked, and the view was exactly the same. And from deep, deep down in the bowels of the hell below him he could hear the lyrics and voices of Britney Spears and Justin Timberlake being blasted out of some massive speaker.

'AAAAAWWWWWGGGGG!' he gurgled, as the reality of his predicament suddenly hit him. He grabbed the wires that went into his arm and yanked them out, then the ones in his back, his head and his legs, before finally taking a deep breath and doing the other one; but then he was gone, his body suddenly sucked from him, and he was hurtling backwards down a chute. He grabbed frantically at the sides, but they were too covered in baked bean slime to give any purchase. Then, as suddenly as it began, the claustrophobia of the chute vanished into a silence as Newo found himself falling through the air.

'AAAAAWWWWGGGG!' he screamed again as he splashed into a cold, dark pool of circulating sewage. He thrashed about in the chods and spluttered and fought as a current tried to drag him under. The force was too strong, though, and his arms gave way as he was sucked under and sent off down another chute, this time completely submerged in darkness and total silence. He grabbed and fought the walls, desperately gasping for breath. The chute seemed to last an eternity, but just as Newo's unconscious brain took over to calm him down before his breath ran out, he was shot out into the blinding daytime sky, landing with a painful splash on the circular gravel court of a sewage processing plant. He lay panting, naked, on his back, fighting with his eyes to look up at the bright sky above, but all he could make out was the rotating spreader arm as it made another rotation and squirted him all over in filth. 'I'm alive,' he thought.

All of a sudden an enormous grizzly bear jumped out of nowhere and started viciously attacking him, clawing and biting at his head. Newo fought back, kicking and biting, but it was useless. The bear picked him up by the thigh and carried him off through a field of stinging nettles and thistles. Newo shrieked in agony as each vicious thorn and stinger bounced off his torn white skin. He was then set upon by a swarm of killer bees, which forced the bear to drop him and run off, before being dipped in hot marmite and finally rescued and taken back to the *Knobachaneza* by Amorphous and Titty.

'We did it, Titty!' exclaimed Amorphous as he and Titty watched over their patient. 'We rescued him.'

'From the bear and the killer bees?' asked Titty.

'From the Matewix,' replied Amorphous.

Newo was once again wired up all over. He was completely naked, bar a handkerchief Stitch had kindly put over his unwaning erection, and his body was covered from head to toe in cocktail sticks as if he were some great party snack. All around him the walls of the *Knobachaneza* throbbed with a psoriasis of monitors and wires and lights and dials.

Tommy came over. 'He's looking good, captain,' he said, prodding Newo's chest with a stick. 'His heart rate's up a bit, but he's doing OK.'

Amorphous smiled and strained his neck towards the ECG monitor. 'I can't see anything in there, Tommy,' he said, tapping the screen with his index finger and adjusting his glasses.

'Perhaps it's the … sunglasses, sir,' replied Tommy.

Amorphous nodded and moved back. 'Perhaps, perhaps. That is not the question, though, is it?'

Tommy looked blank. 'No, sir … but I'm sure you're going to tell me what is,' he replied.

'The question is, Tommy: the night of the long knives?'

'Yes' replied Tommy.

'How long were the knives?'

Tommy shook his head. ' I don't … I don't know, to be honest.'

'He's waking up!' yelled Titty.

Everyone looked towards the sleeping corpse. 'No, sorry, sorry, false alarm.' The others drew back a little. 'His knob twitched a bit, that's all.'

'Perhaps he is dreaming, Titty. Perhaps he is having a dream so real that he cannot wake from it – a bit like Phallus going down the rabbit hole, Titty.'

Titty smiled nervously and moved away from Amorphous. 'Perhaps,' she replied, and left the room.

Newo lay on the operating table for three days before Tommy and Shrew removed the cocktail sticks from his body and poured a cup of cold coffee over his face to wake him up. Newo jumped into life and shook off the coffee.

'What's going on? Where am I? Am I alive?' he shrieked as he opened his eyes to see the two figures looming over him with their dripping cup.

'The question is not "Am I alive?"' came a booming voice as Amorphous strolled into the room. 'The question is "W*hen* am I alive?" Ouch ... bastard!' he shouted as he walked square into the door frame. He held his nose in pain.

'When am I alive?' asked Newo.

Amorphous wiped his nose a little. 'As far as we know, the year is 2020, like my vision,' explained Amorphous as he looked for blood but couldn't see anything because it was too dark. 'To our knowledge robots took over the world some time at the beginning of the 21st century. At around the same time man created the television show *Robot Wars*. At first it was a simple battle of badly constructed cake tins with lawn mower engines and shopping trolley wheels all fighting for Philippa Forrester's approval. But the robots progressed, Newo. They started evolving ... evolving spinning blades and big choppers. After the sixth war the programme was axed by BBC2 and moved over to Channel Five. This is when it began to take a sinister turn. Some roboteers spent so long locked away in their bedrooms communicating with no one but their goldfish and men posing as girls on the internet, working night and day on their robots, that they realized communicating with their robots was the only way they could survive ... So some did ... By the eighth war the robots were controlling themselves. By the ninth war the robots were doing the filming and editing, and by the tenth war there was no contest. Robots had taken over the world.'

Newo looked shocked. 'What happened to Philippa?' he asked.

'She was lost, Newo ... like so many others.' Newo shook his head and tried to hold back the tears. 'Those who didn't die went underground. They excavated disused badger setts and rabbit holes and lived in them for years, eating grass and foraging up trees for fruits. Eventually all their tunnels met up and they vanished further beneath the surface until their connections with the sun were finally severed altogether ... Now, Newo, they all live together in a place we call Llanfairpwllgwyngyllgogerychwyrn-drobwllllantysiliogogogocock.'

Newo swung his legs off the edge of the bed and hung his head, shaking it. 'It's tewwible ... tewwible.' As he stood up and stretched, he noticed Titty staring at him. He squinted at her to get focus. 'My clothes!' he suddenly burst out, realizing his manhood was on display. 'Where are my clothes?' He grabbed his member and crouched over it.

'Titty, stop staring!' shouted Amorphous. 'Tommy, get the man some clothes. We're not in the Matewix now.' Tommy threw Newo a towel and went to grab him something to wear. 'And get him one of those modesty pouches ... he took the blue pill, goddamn it!' he shouted after him. 'Rest now, Newo. You need to rest.' Amorphous lay Newo back on the bed and tucked him in. 'I'll show you my ship tomorrow,' he explained, kissed Newo on the forehead and left, grabbing Titty by the arm. 'Come on, Titty. Stop staring at his cock.'

Newo had no idea what time it was when he woke again. He looked at his watch but it wasn't there. He sat up and felt his head. His hair had been brushed and trimmed a little, but it was still very long. His beard had been trimmed into a fashionable goatee and his mutton chops were almost gone.

'Come, Newo, I have much to show you,' said Amorphous as he came into the room.

Newo climbed off the bed and followed him. 'Where awe we going, Amowphous?' he asked.

They went out the door and up a flight of thick oak stairs.

'This is my ship, Newo, the *Knobachaneza*. It's a late fifties' Russian milk float.'

Newo looked about in awe. It was vast and green from floor to floor, wall to wall, in badly painted sheet steel. Among the green were red bits where the paint had rusted off, and there were pipes going everywhere, some smoking, others rusting.

At the top of the stairs Amorphous stopped to admire his ship while Newo caught up. 'It is powered by a 900cc motorbike engine with two Hayter Lawn Mower 250 petrol engine boosters.'

Newo was impressed and nodded accordingly. 'How fast can she go?' he asked.

Amorphous grinned proudly. 'She can push eight miles an hour downhill!'

Newo looked suitably awed. 'Come on, Newo, enough talk of machines. Let me introduce you to my crew.'

At the top of the stairs and through a door were his crew. They hung about looking cool, waiting to be introduced. 'This is, well, there's Siphon, Epoch, the small one's Shrew and over there that's Stitch, she makes a good cup of tea, Digger and his brother Tommy. And of course Titty.'

Titty smiled at Newo in a most seductive manner. Newo blushed a little and tried to smile back. 'My teeth!' he said, grabbing his mouth.

'What?' asked Amorphous. 'What is it?'

Newo looked up, horrified. 'I just caught their weflection in the miwwor ... my teeth, Amorphous ... they'we bwight owange.'

Amorphous patted him on the back and smiled. 'My dear Newo, you spent the first twenty-five years of your life immersed in a solution of baked beans and alphabet spaghetti. Like all those we release, your teeth are stained by the tomato sauce within which the beans and pasta shapes exist. So the question, my dear boy, is not "Why are my teeth orange?" The question is "When will they not be orange?"'

Newo nodded. 'Yes, that's the question, definitely.'

'In about two years,' replied Amorphous. Newo shook his head and dropped his hand from his mouth. 'My dear boy, think what it's like for Janet Street Porter. Now we must go to Llanfairpwllgwyngyllgogerychwyrndrobwllllantysiliogogogocock. Tommy, fire her up. Let's get to Llanfairpwllgwyngyllgogerychwyrndrobwllllantysiliogogogocock.'

The great hulking beast fired into life and chugged its way down the M4, over the Severn bridge and off towards Llanfairpwllgwyngyllgogerychwyrndrobwllllantysiliogogogocock at over six miles an hour.

'Now, Newo … your training.'

Newo was sat down in a dentist's chair. Two small television screens were put in front of his face, and between each screen and each of his two eyes were placed the cardboard bits from two toilet rolls so that

he could see a separate screen with each eye. A pair
of headphones was put over his ears and a couple of
little electronic pulse pads were attached to his
forehead to try and help him lose weight while he was
training.

'Are you ready for your training, Newo?' asked
Amorphous. 'When are you ready for you training?'

'Pwetty much now,' replied Newo.

'Then it shall begin.'

Newo suddenly jerked in agony. He grabbed the
headphones and tried to pull them off, but they
wouldn't budge. He thrashed about for a while,
clutching his head and shaking, but eventually gave
up and watched the pictures on the television screen.

It was incredible. He watched for hours and hours:
mud wrestle after mud wrestle, Sumo fight after
Sumo fight. He watched playground punch-ups and
conker matches. For two straight hours his brain
absorbed almost nothing of any use for his own
defence; he could neither attack nor defend himself
against anyone except perhaps a Brownie. But he
wasn't put off. His brain kept taking it, absorbing

almost nothing for another three quarters of an hour.

Amorphous came in to watch. 'He's incredible,' remarked Tommy. 'Look at these brain patterns, Amorphous.' He pointed to a screen, but Amorphous was unable to locate it – he just looked about a bit and pretended.

'That's incredible,' he said, looking back towards Newo.

'He's been watching for two and three-quarter hours straight, and taken in almost nothing.'

Amorphous lent over him and smiled. 'He is the Number Two.'

'I think he's ready now,' said Tommy ten minutes later. 'I think he's ready to go into the program.'

Amorphous seemed to agree. 'OK,' he said. 'Load the program.'

Shrew came in to help and went looking for one of his tapes. 'Start him on this one,' he said as he handed it to Tommy.

'What? *A Fireman's Guide to Lesbianism*?'

Shrew looked embarrassed and whipped the tape

out of Tommy's hand. 'No, this one.' He handed him another.

'*Badger Watching for the Faint-hearted.*'

Shrew nodded. 'That's the one.'

'Perhaps not,' boomed Amorphous. 'How about a bit of mud wrestling?'

Tommy agreed. Shrew got him the tape and he put it into the tape recorder and pressed Play. 'It'll take about six minutes to load and then it probably won't work,' he explained. 'These old Spectrums aren't up to much any more.'

Thirty-six minutes later they were in. Newo was standing in a blue space with nothing but a green inflatable paddling pool full of mud. He looked about but there was nothing but blue as far as the eye could see. He looked himself over. He was wearing a pair of Speedos and nothing else. He began to feel slightly uneasy. Amorphous appeared. All eighteen stone of him. He was dressed in a tiny pair of red Speedos and a pair of pink goggles.

'Where am I?' asked Newo.

'This,' replied Amorphous, 'is a practise program.'

'But where is it?' begged Newo.

'It is in your head, Newo. Like a dream world. It is a computer-generated program that is played into your head. You believe it to be real, don't you, Newo?' Newo nodded. 'What is real, Newo?' Newo thought for a moment and gave up. 'That is the question, is it not?' continued Amorphous. 'When is real, Newo?'

Newo shrugged. 'I don't know,' he replied.

'You will understand, Newo ... you will.' Amorphous went over to the paddling pool and climbed in. 'Come, Newo. Let your training begin.'

Newo was hesitant but knew he had to do it. He'd never mud-wrestled a man before, especially not such a large one dressed only in Speedos. Newo stepped in and smiled at Amorphous nervously. Amorphous adopted a fairly predatory stance and looked hard at Newo, who felt very thin and white, because he was.

'Is this entirely necessawy, Amowphous?' he asked one more time.

Amorphous grinned like a shit-eater and shouted

'Go!' He lunged at Newo and grabbed him around the torso. Newo tried to tear Amorphous's arms off him, but the great man was much stronger and he pulled him sideways down into the mud. Newo thrashed about and kicked, trying to get back up, but Amorphous grabbed his inner thigh and started swinging him round the inside of the paddling pool. Newo managed to get hold of his arm, though, and forced him to release his grip. He flew backwards into the side of the pool and immediately sprang back up.

Amorphous laughed excitedly. 'You see, Newo, it's fun, isn't it?' he boomed, and then dived at his opponent. Newo tried to dodge, but Amorphous caught him by the foot and reeled him in. Newo tried to kick him off, but it was pointless. Amorphous got him by the shoulders, pulling him over his body until Newo lay on his back on top of Amorphous. Newo jerked his shoulders about frantically and kicked, but it was no use, he was stuck in Amorphous's vice-like grip.

Amorphous lifted his mouth to Newo's ear. 'You can do better than that, Newo.'

'You're too stwong,' replied Newo, panting.

'You think my muscles have anything to do with strength in here, Newo? You think that is mud you're wrestling in?'

Newo looked slightly horrified. 'I hope it is,' he replied.

Amorphous shook his head. 'Newo, Newo ... use your head, Newo. You can beat me, Newo.'

Amorphous released him and Newo slumped forward into the mud. 'I can't,' he wailed.

'Don't think you can, Newo. Know you can.'

'But I don't think I can, Amowphous.'

Amorphous suddenly leaped on Newo again, this time dominating him from above. Newo lay flat, face down. Amorphous sat hard on his back and grabbed for his arms. He got them and pulled them back.

'Aaagggghhh! My cock!' shouted Newo. 'Aaagggghhh! Amowphous, don't forget I took the blue pill.'

Amorphous grinned. 'Well then, you must release it, Newo. Release it from the Speedos.'

Newo found a sudden burst of energy and leaped

free of Amorphous and out of the pool. He ran as fast as he could into the blueness, with sloppy mud dripping from his body.

'Where are you going, Newo?' shouted Amorphous after him.

'Away fwom you, you big homo,' Newo shouted back.

Amorphous shook his head and smiled to himself. 'So young,' he said. 'Tommy, load the Morris dancing.'

Half an hour later Newo was an experienced Morris dancer, and as a result understood a few more facets of life. Amorphous was pleased with him.

'You learn relatively quickly, Newo,' he remarked. Newo nodded nervously, trying to keep a safe distance from the man. 'Tommy, I think it's time to load the dump program.'

Tommy looked excited. Shrew rushed out of the room and into the kitchen area to tell the others. 'They're loading the dump program!' he shouted. The others jumped to their feet and followed him.

'Would anyone like a cup of tea?' called Stitch after them.

The maypole that separated Newo from Amorphous suddenly vanished and was replaced by a toilet and a table with various foodstuffs on it. Amorphous walked over to the table. 'Newo ... my dear boy ... here we have a selection of foods: some figs, a few cloves of garlic, a couple of bowls of prunes, a kilo of bran, a bar or two of Ex-Lax, a pint of castor oil and a bowl of two-week-old *moules marinières*.' Newo cast an eye over the food. 'When you enter the Matewix you will not have time to use any toilet facilities. If you shit in the Matewix, you shit in the real world too. And then Digger has to clear it all up. So as part of your training, Newo, you must learn not to shit.' Amorphous picked a mussel out of the bowl, broke the shell apart and threw the bivalve down his throat.

'I'm allergic to shellfish, though,' explained Newo.

'I know you are, Newo. But you must try one.' Amorphous handed him a mussel dripping with stagnant white wine and bits of soggy onion. 'The mussel does not exist, Newo. Remember that. Free

COLEG LLANDRILLO COLLEGE
LIBRARY RESOURCE CENTRE
CANOLFAN ADNODDAU LLYFRGELL

your mind, Newo. You must free your mind … and then you can eat the mussel.'

Newo looked hard at the mussel. Amorphous picked up a bowl of prunes in syrup and poured the lot down his throat. 'What about the stones?' asked Newo.

Amorphous burped. 'You think the prunes are real, Newo? Hmmm. You think the stones exist?'

Newo looked at the mussel. 'OK, free your mind,' he said to himself. He slowly prised the shell apart; inside the fleshy orangeness of a fresh mussel had turned dark and putrid. 'The mussel isn't weal,' he said, shut his eyes, took a deep breath and swallowed. He winced and craned his neck as the mussel slid down his throat, but popped his head back in when it reached his stomach.

'You see, Newo, it's not so bad.' Newo appeared to disagree. 'You must eat more, Newo. Eat the whole bowl. Then you must eat the garlic, the figs and both bars of Ex-Lax.' Amorphous handed him the pint glass of castor oil. 'You must drink this also, Newo.'

COLEG LLANDRILLO COLLEGE
LIBRARY RESOURCE CENTRE
CANOLFAN ADNODDAU LLYFRGELL

The Matewix

Newo took the glass and looked at it with terror. 'The glass isn't weal,' he muttered to himself.

CHAPTER THREE

THE ANCIENT GEEKS

A few hours later, when Digger had finished clearing up the mess from the dump program, he was back at the controls. The *Knobachaneza* was nearing Llanfairpwllgwyngyllgogerychwyrndrobwllllantysiliogogocock and Digger was steering it through the back roads of west Wales towards the motherland. Newo watched in fascination out of the window.

'This is the *Knobachaneza* calling Llanfairpwllgwyngyllgogerychwyrndrobwllllantysiliogogogocock, do you read me on this frequency?' asked Digger down the radio.

'This is Llanfairpwllgwyngyllgogerychwyrndrobwllllantysiliogogogocock,' came the reply. 'We read you loud and clear, *Knobber*. Welcome home.'

Digger grinned with excitement. 'It's good to be

home, Llanfairpwllgwyngyllgogerychwyrndrobwllllantysiliogogogocock. Are we clear for arrival?'

'You sure are, *Knobber*. Parking bay 7.'

The huge mesh gates of Llanfairpwllgwyngyllgogerychwyrndrobwllllantysiliogogogocock Station
drew open and the enormous milk float drove in and
parked at bay 7.

Newo looked in awe out of the window. 'So this
is Llanfadubpbwpgygbbbbbllllllllihttpwwwbbc/cock,
is it?'

'It sure is, Newo,' replied Digger, 'but we
pronounce it Llanfairpwllgwyngyllgogerychwyrndrobwllllantysiliogogogocock. It doesn't have the
"BBC" followed by the forward slash at the end.'

'Hmm,' replied Newo. 'So it's more Llanfaiwpwll-
gwyngyllgogewychwywndwobwllllantysiliogogogo-
cock?'

'Ish, yes, but with a few less w's and a couple more
r's,' explained Digger as he reversed a bit to
straighten the *Knobachaneza* up.

'You'll get it one day,' interrupted Amorphous.

'Llanfaiwpwllgwyngyllgogewychwyrndrobwllllantysiliogogogocock,' said Newo one more time.

Amorphous smiled. 'You see, Newo. You are the Number Two.'

Digger shut down the *Knobachaneza* and opened the door.

'We're going to need a full charge of the batteries,' instructed Amorphous. 'I want this milk float ready to go in forty-eight hours.'

Digger nodded and jumped out.

'Come, Newo. I'll show you where the locals hang out,' said Amorphous and dragged Newo off by the arm to the main station. Titty followed, while Stitch and Siphon hung back to do the washing up and generally give the place a good once over.

'This is like the Grand Central Station of Carmathenshire,' explained Amorphous as they burst through the doors into the ticket office.

The man behind the ticket counter took one look at Amorphous and shouted across the lobby, 'Call the police, Denzil. It's that loony bloke again.'

Amorphous leaped across the counter and grabbed the ticket salesmen. He fought a little, trying to drop down below the counter so that he could escape. But Amorphous was strong, and lifted him off his feet and over the counter.

The man grabbed at Amorphous's enormous hands, but it was no use. 'Let me go, intit!' he shouted.

Amorphous nutted the man square in the face, chopped him in the neck with an almighty blow of his right hand and snapped his neck with a kick to the head. The man fell limp to the floor. Denzil came running over with his broom to help his ticket-selling friend, but never made it. Titty pulled out a gun and shot him right between the eyes. At that point prospective passengers and the old women who loiter around railway stations because they've nothing better to do began to leave. Titty shot a couple of them, did a cartwheel and broke through a door.

Inside the doorway was a flight of stairs that led down into darkness. Titty went down. 'Come on, Newo,' said Amorphous. 'This is the real Llanfair-pwllgwyngyllgogerychwyrndrobwllllantysiliogogo-gocock (a place we shall refer to simply as "Cock" from now on).' Newo made for the stairs. 'You might have to help me down a bit, though, because it's a bit dark down there and I can't see shit with these damn glasses on.' Amorphous grabbed about for Newo and found his hand. 'My, what soft hands you have, Newo.' Newo smiled nervously in the gloom and began to lead the enormous Amorphous down the steps.

After what seemed like an eternity they reached the bottom, where a pair of candles framed a door. 'This is the doorway to Cock,' explained Titty in a most seductive way.

Newo watched as a slither of sweat slid down her bust and into her latex bosom. 'Is it?' he said in a most dopey fashion. 'Is it weally?'

Titty smiled, turned the door handle and went through.

Inside were more candles and a long stone corridor. Newo led Amorphous down the corridor by the hand. Music boomed off in the distance; Newo listened hard to hear who it was. 'I think that's Bwos, "When Will I Be Famous", isn't it?'

Titty turned and nodded. 'It has been number 1 in the Welsh charts ever since its release in 1988,' she said.

'It's the theme tune to our struggle in Cock,' interrupted Amorphous.

Newo was slightly surprised and tried to forgive them their strange underground ways.

An enormous cavern opened up at the end of the corridor. It was lit yellow by candles and street lights that had obviously been stolen from Haverfordwest. Newo looked out over the cave from a balcony formed by the rock. Stalagmites or stalactites hung from the ceiling and dripped moisture onto the vast village of people and machinery below. The cave must have measured 45 metres across and was buzzing with almost thirty people.

'Behold Cock!' said Amorphous, facing the wall.

'It's over there,' whispered Titty.

Amorphous turned round to try and see it.

Newo noticed a sign that read Caerphilly Cheese Factory but chose to ignore it. 'Er, why exactly are we here?' he asked.

'We are here to find the Cheese Maker, Newo. You cannot destroy the Matewix without the Cheese Maker.'

'Who is he?' asked Newo.

Amorphous released his grasp from Newo's hand and did one of his masterly strolls. 'When the Matewix was created, darling Newo, it was the work of one man. His name was Archie Text. He empowered several people and programs with power over the Matewix, to act as a safeguard for his own survival – to protect himself, Newo, against the machines. It was his understanding that these people's personalities were so far removed from each other's that they would never meet and conspire against the Matewix. And thus never destroy it. He didn't want it destroyed. The Cheese Maker, Newo, is one of these people. He is such an arsehole that it is unlikely any of the other "special programs" will ever cross his path, or indeed want to.'

'So where is he now?' asked Newo.

'The Cheese Maker was once a child of Cock. However, he was taken from us and inserted into the

Matewix. The Agent Provocateurs captured him, and the Bentanals took his ship. With his body and his mind reunited he was inserted into the Matewix to make quality cheeses for a very clever and very vicious program called the Merrill Lynch. He now exists permanently in the Matewix, locked away in a dairy.'

'So why look for him here?' queried Newo. 'Why not look for him in the Matewix?'

Amorphous nodded at the intelligence of the question. 'The Merrill Lynch is a very clever program; he is half American, half Argentinian and two-thirds Dutch. He is thus ignorant, unreasonable and ultimately bad at making cheese. For this reason he needs a cheese maker. He is good at hiding, though. Indeed, not even the Mystic Mog knows where he can be found. Therefore we must do outside the Matewix what we cannot do within.'

Newo thought hard. 'And what is that?'

'Find the Cheese Maker in body, if not in mind.' Newo nodded understandingly. 'He has a birthmark, Newo. It is a very embarrassing one. Only two people know where it is – his wife and his wife's gynaecologist … oh, and his wife's best friend Moira, and Moira's husband Dennis and Valerie Maplesyrup, editor of the Cock WI magazine, but apart from them no one else. So in order to find the body of the Cheese Maker in the power station, so that we may disconnect him physically, we must first discover the nature of his embarrassing birthmark.' Newo looked out across Cock and tried to understand just what the heckety heck Amorphous was talking about. 'Come now, Newo and Titty. Let us rest for a while and then discover the true nature of the Cheese Maker's birthmark.'

Siphon sweated as he waited for DCI Smiff to appear. He eventually did, and called Siphon through to an interview room. 'Hmm … Mr Nixon … hmm … I can only assume you would like a coffee, Mr Nixon …hmm.' Siphon looked at him and lit a cigarette. 'Take a seat, Mr … hmm … Nixon,' ordered Smiff.

'The name's Siphon,' protested Siphon. 'Milk and six sugars, if you don't mind.'

Smiff smiled wryly to himself. 'Yes, of course, Mr

Siphon. Two coffees, please, Beacham,' he instructed to his sidekick and sat down. 'Mr Siphon – if indeed it's OK to call you that – hmm ... yyeesss ... hmm. You are wil...ling to make a deeeeal with me, I under...stand. Hmm.'

Siphon sat back in his chair to try and look cool, and put his feet up on the table. 'Yes, perhaps,' he said coolly.

Smiff sniffed and looked at Siphon's enormous feet. 'You have, er, poop on your shoe, Mr Siphon ... hmm ... dog poop.'

Siphon smiled. 'You know as well as I do that the poop is not real, Smiff.'

Smiff smiled back. 'But you'd like it to be real, wouldn't you, Mr Siphon?'

Siphon nodded and thanked Beacham for his coffee. He sipped it and smiled again. 'This coffee is not real. But I like it.'

Smiff looked at him in disgust. 'It's Mellow Birds, Mr Siphon ... hmm ... with six sugars in it. Certainly not real.'

Siphon sat forward. 'I like it, though. I like it a lot.

It reminds me of good things – of good food and good times. It reminds me of staying up late and watching crap on the television. Of getting up in the morning to bacon and eggs, of washing up with Fairy Liquid – all those things I can't do in this stupid real world. Stitch does all the washing up round here, and I don't want it. I want back in. I want back in: hooked up, fed slop, brainfed with drivel. I want it, Mr Smiff. I want back into the Matewix.'

Smiff drew his hands together into a praying position and looked at Siphon. 'And in return for your … reinsertion … you will give me …?'

'Amorphous,' replied Siphon. 'I will give you Amorphous.'

Smiff sat back, smiling. 'I think we can do something, Mr, er, Siphon.'

'And I want to go back as a woman. A big woman with enormous milk churns for tits and a great big fanny. And I want to be bi-curious and have a bedsit in Telford. And I want an old Morris Minor and one of those sofas made of emerald green PVC that goes round a corner rather than being flush up against the wall.' Smiff didn't appear to have a problem with any of this. 'And I want to run a day care centre for elderly victims of Alzheimer's disease. And keep geese. And have a bath instead of a shower, once a month. And I want a bike with stabilizers and a paddling pool and a toy garage and a Barbie with the stable block and Ken stable boy kit. And a Barbie Mini and a cuddly donkey and a Candyfloss Maker and a face paint kit and a zircon-encrusted tiara and a packet of Refreshers and a Baby Alive doll that shits itself ... Oh, and a couple of blocks of Caerphilly thrown in for good measure.'

Smiff nodded and looked up at Beacham. 'Mad as a brush,' Beacham mouthed back.

Smiff nodded and turned to Siphon. 'Hmm ... yess, Mr Siphon, I don't see a problem with any of those things. Hmm ... the Barbie Mini has been discontinued for some time, but I'm sure we can find a replacement.'

Siphon sat back and smiled. 'It's a pleasure doing business with you, Mr Smiff.'

* * *

They began the search for the mark of the Cheese Maker. Some said it was like a map of Merthyr Tydfil on his right buttock; others said it was more like a picture of a watering can on his cock. What Amorphous, Titty and Newo did know for sure was that the man obviously hid some hugely embarrassing stain within his groin area, and – the destruction of the Matewix and the salvation of humanity aside – they wanted to know what it was. They were struggling, though. The Cheese Maker's wife was away on a business trip, and her gynaecologist simply refused to divulge professional secrets, even though Amorphous kicked him about a bit. Newo had suggested allowing him to do an examination on Titty in exchange for the secret, but it turned out that he'd only reveal the secret if he were allowed a full internal examination of Newo, and Newo declined, claiming that he was still sore from the whelk removal.

'Punctured by the fork, eh?' suggested the gynae-cologist. Newo became embarrassed and nodded a little. 'I've seen it so many times before. Would you like me to take a proper look?' he suggested in the vain hope of widening the circle of his friends.

'I could help you,' suggested Amorphous.

But Newo got scared and ran away. Titty followed, leaving Amorphous with no clues, no answers, just a slightly dodgy gynaecologist and an operating table. 'Actually, I've got a sore bum,' said Amorphous, checking that Newo and Titty were completely gone.

The gynaecologist smiled. 'Would you like me to examine it for you?'

Amorphous nodded and climbed onto the operating table. 'Quite a little cottage industry you've got going here,' he said.

'Yes, it is,' replied the gynaecologist and shut his eyes.

After a little detective work by Titty and Newo, and several dead members of the Cock WI later, it turned out that the Cheese Maker's birthmark was an almost perfect picture of the Battle of El Alamein being played out on his arse, with Rommel as his balls and Monty as his old chap. Titty and Newo ran back to tell Amorphous the news, but he was nowhere to be found. Indeed they didn't see him again until that evening.

Amorphous was in council with the Cock elders. 'We are in grave danger, Amorphous. It seems that Cock is being descended on by an army of Bentanals. It is thought that they'll reach the cheese factory on the outer rim of Cock within twenty-four hours.' The ginger-haired councillor woman sat down to add gravity to her news.

'The question is not, then, "Are we going to be attacked?" The question is "*When* are we going to be attacked?"' said Amorphous.

'In twenty-four hours,' reiterated the woman.

'Yes, yes, of course,' replied Amorphous.

'It is very serious, Amorphous – perhaps a greater threat to Cock and the cheese factory than there has ever been before,' said a large, greying man wearing a brightly coloured cloak.

Amorphous strolled about, fairly deep in thought. 'To be or not to be ... that is the question ... This foul and hanging firmament ... Perchance to dream ... hmmm ... Wherefore art thou, Cock? ... We must make contact with Mystic Mog. It is our only chance.'

Some of the elders seemed to disagree. 'How, Amorphous, is a domestic cat going to help us now? What godly powers does such a creature hold that you regard its worth so paramount to the salvation of the humanity of planet Earth?'

'The man's quite insane!' shouted a much younger chap across the room.

'Quiet,' shouted the ginger elder.

Amorphous span on one foot to face the man. 'My sanity is not why I am here, comrade. We are not all here today to bring such trivial matters into question. There are greater forces at work than mere personality.'

'Well, explain the use of a domestic cat in the salvation of all mankind, please, Amorphous,' ordered the grey-haired elder.

'The cat is ... not of this earth. She is a program created in the early stages of the first Matewix. She was a flawed program, though, riddled with viruses. Archie Text, the creator of the Matewix, didn't have the heart to put her down, despite her various respiratory complaints and her constant vomiting, so he released her into the Matewix as one of the "special programs", empowering her with various insights and abilities. It also seems that she spent so long sitting on Archie Text's lap, purring and watching his computer while he created the Matewix, that she knows what happens in it – like a game, and she knows how to get to the end,' explained Amorphous.

'What an absolute pile of wank!' shouted the younger comrade. 'The man's quite insane.'

The elders nodded and considered. 'And what of this Newo? You say he's a Number Two,' said the ginger elder.

'*The* Number Two,' corrected Amorphous. 'I believe he is *the* Number Two.'

'You believe, you believe!' shouted the young captain.

'My prerogative here is not to be believed,

comrade,' replied Amorphous.' My prerogative is to believe.'

'And what makes you so sure this man is the Number Two?' asked the grey-haired elder.

'Your honour, I have seen the way he moves. It is god-like: his thigh, his chest … he mud wrestles no-handed! I am in no doubt that Newo is the Number Two.'

'Interesting. And how do you plan for this Newo to destroy the Matewix, Amorphous?' asked the grey-haired elder again.

'I do not plan anything, your honour. What will be, will be. I need not plan for Newo to destroy the Matewix. Newo has already destroyed the Matewix.'

'Well, then, why are we having this discussion?' asked the ginger woman.

Amorphous smiled to himself. 'Do I detect, from your position on this earth as a *woman*, your ladyship, that you don't quite "get" complicated plots because you're too busy thinking about your relationships? And the whole concept of the Matewix that was so carefully conceived by Archie Text and the Noamchomsky Brothers has flown completely over your head?'

The ginger lady nodded. 'Well, it does get a bit complicated, I have to be honest,' she replied.

'Would you like me to explain the concept of a Matewix, your ladyship?'

The ginger lady looked horrified at the thought of having to listen to Amorphous explaining anything complicated when he made explaining even the simplest thing so dramatically obscure. 'No,' she replied, 'just take your milk float off and find that cat.'

Amorphous nodded. 'Mystic Mog,' he mused.

'Yes, that cat,' replied the woman.

'Just one more thing, Amorphous, before you go,' said the grey-haired elder. 'How are you to understand the cat when you find it? After all, it is a cat!'

Amorphous nodded. 'The cat does not even speak a language, your honour. It simply meows a lot. Indeed I have spent many hours stroking the pussy and have, as yet, failed to make sense of even a single

one of its noises. But Newo, your honour ...
Newo will understand the cat. He is the Number
Two.'

The elders all seemed to understand. The only
person who didn't was the young captain, who shook
his head in disbelief. 'I cannot believe you are
swallowing this shit! The man's a loony. He should be
sectioned!' he burst out.

'*Silence*, comrade!' shouted the grey-haired elder.
'Now you must go forth, Amorphous. Go forth with
Godspeed and contact the cat.'

'First I must find the Cheese Maker,' replied
Amorphous.

'What? The bloke with the Battle of El Alamein on
his arse?' queried the grey-haired elder.

'Yes, your honour.'

'What on earth for? He's a complete arse head.'

'Sir, the Cheese Maker's mind exists now
exclusively within the Matewix. He is ...'

'Oh, just go, Amorphous, go! Stop blathering on
about the bloody Matewix.' Amorphous turned and
left. 'And make sure you've got a good speech ready

72

for the party tonight,' shouted the grey-haired man after him.

At midnight a great gong was banged. The sound echoed around the vast 40-metre chamber of Cock, and its thirty or so inhabitants gathered together to party. First there were speeches. The grey-haired elder said something about sanitation and non-payment of Alcove Tax, before letting Amorphous step forward and take centre stage.

'Now hear me, people of Cock!' he began.

'You're facing the wall, Amorphous,' whispered the elder.

Amorphous span round and shouted '*Cock!*' so loud that the sound bounced off the walls and echoed 'Cocococococococococock' off into the darkness. 'We face a threat here tonight,' he shouted, lifting his arms into the air. Some of the people in the crowd booed him, others heckled him with 'Twat!' and 'Wanker!', but he ignored them. 'We are under attack, people. There gathers together above us a great army. A great army of Bentanals bent on destroying us!' People began to chat among themselves, bored with what Amorphous had to say. 'But we are greater than them. They have tried to conquer us before, but they have failed. And they will fail again. Cock must rise up ... rise up and fight the Bentanals like cocks.'

Amorphous span in triumph and threw his arms up in the air. Everyone in the crowd ignored him, talking among themselves, except for one teenager who just shouted 'cock' at him.

The grey-haired elder stepped in. 'That's probably enough, Amorphous. The cock gag may be getting a bit cheesy now as well.'

Amorphous nodded and stood down.

Then the music began, bursting forth from a great speaker. It was a Ronan Keating song, and everybody danced like girls for the rest of the night.

CHAPTER FOUR

UNORTHODOX GEEKS

The *Knobachaneza* cleared the Severn Bridge and headed back down the M4. The sign westbound at Junction 12 stated, 'For the Oracle use Junction 11.' It was quite clearly a sign to the Oracle shopping mall in Reading, but Amorphous suspected it was a hidden message as to the whereabouts of Mystic Mog.

'It is time, Newo.'

Newo was enjoying a cup of tea on the main deck of the *Knobber* and talking to Stitch about her 'welationship pwoblems' after she'd thrown a blob strop at Shrew for leaving his towel on the floor after his bath.

'It is time to take you back into the Matewix.'

Newo stood up. 'The Matewix, Amowphous?' he asked.

'Yes, Newo, the Matewix. We have work to do. First we must find Mystic Mog, and then we must find the Cheese Maker. Titty, Stitch, Shrew, Epoch, Siphon – get ready, we're going in.'

The crew leaped into action. They pressed various buttons on computers and looked at various monitors before attaching various things to themselves.

'Will you be wearing the leather dress or the PVC catsuit, Titty?' asked Tommy as his fingers bounced off the computer keyboard.

'The ... the ... Actually I've got a lovely new Laura Ashley dress. Could I wear that?'

The boys all looked disappointed, except for Amorphous. Tommy tapped some keys and pretended to be confused. 'To be honest, Titty, I'm not sure you can. I'm not sure I can load it.' Just then Tommy spilled some tea over his computer. He leaped up and shook it off, holding the keyboard upside down so that the tea could drain out. 'Shit, shit, shit,' he cursed.

'Is it all right, Tommy?' asked Amorphous.

'I think so,' he replied, wiping it with a tissue.

'Good. Get us in there.'

The crew strapped themselves into their various chairs and Amorphous whispered something about the Laura Ashley dress into Tommy's ear before he too strapped in.

Stitch was the first to appear in the empty whore-house. She was wearing the rear end of a pantomime horse. She had dark brown furry legs with floppy foam hooves and a pair of braces holding them up over her bare breasts. Next in was Epoch wearing a two-piece magenta shell suit and a pair of large yellow wellies. After that came Shrew dressed in full bondage gear with an orange in his mouth. Then came Siphon dressed as a big 'wet nurse' with enormous milk churn tits and a great big fanny. And finally Titty wearing a barbed-wire G-string and bra, Amorphous dressed as normal, and last of all Newo dressed in Titty's brand new Laura Ashley dress with his erection sticking out.

'I think perhaps spilling that cup of tea on the

keyboard may have caused a glitch in the program, Amorphous,' said Tommy down the phone.

The crew looked at themselves in horror, except for Siphon who was very happy and felt his enormous bosom.

'I think perhaps you're right, Tommy,' replied Amorphous down the phone. 'Although Newo does look rather ravishing in that dress,' he continued.

Newo blushed red and fell back a bit behind Titty.

'I'm not sure I can really work in this barbed wire,' said Titty. 'It's digging into my soft pert breasts and hurting my peach of a bum.'

'Well, there's no time, Titty. You will have to cope.'

Amorphous led the way out of the whorehouse to a waiting Vauxhall Astra. The crew were nervous. They looked about a lot, checking for Agent Provocateurs. Titty sat down gently in the driving seat, careful not to prick her pretty little bottom on the dirty, sharp spikes of the barbed wire. Amorphous got in the passenger side and Newo climbed in the back. Siphon joined him, but only after he'd done something unusual. He'd pulled his phone from his bra and dropped it into a trash can that was coincidentally placed right next to the car. Shrew stayed back in the whorehouse to guard the equipment, and Epoch and Stitch guarded the door. The car pulled out into the dark back streets and made its way through Reading towards the shopping centre.

It was a Thursday evening and raining heavily. The crew were hopelessly lost. Amorphous had been reading the map upside down and they'd ended up somewhere near Slough.

'Where are we, Tommy?' he asked down the phone.

'I don't know, sir. It appears that there is a gap in the Matewix between Reading and the M25, and you're in it.'

Amorphous huffed.

'I said we should have taken that left back near Wallingford,' said Siphon.

'Look, you want to navigate?' shouted Amorphous, throwing the map into the back at Siphon.

'Well, you'd better decide what we're going to do

because I'm not driving round in circles all night with these barbs pinching my soft pink nipples,' said Titty angrily.

Just then a marmalade-coloured cat ran across the road in front of the car, causing Titty to hit the brakes and skid. There was a frozen silence inside.

'There she is,' whispered Amorphous. 'Mystic Mog.'

They stared motionless as the cat made its way through a front gate and jumped up through an open ground floor window.

'We must follow,' ordered Amorphous, opening his door and getting out. 'Come, Newo … It is time to meet Mystic Mog.'

Amorphous and Newo walked up to the house. Newo looked about, still embarrassed about his dress and his unwaning erection that seemed so accentuated by it. Amorphous knocked on the door and an elderly woman answered.

'Hello,' she said.

'We are here to see Mystic Mog,' said Amorphous, putting his hand on the door to hold it open.

The woman squinted at him; he squinted back. 'I

don't know what you're talking about, young man. There's no Misty Mog here. I think you've got the wrong house. Have you tried the Dolbys next door? They've got a cat.'

Suddenly the woman slumped to the floor, dead. Newo looked down at her, frozen with shock. She had a bullet hole in her forehead, from which was oozing a pool of blood. He turned round to see Titty standing by the car in her barbed-wire bra and panties, blowing the smoke from her steaming gun. He began to get a bit scared.

'She was an Agent Provocateur, Newo.'

Newo nodded, sort of, and followed nervously as Amorphous stepped over the old woman into a rather tastelessly decorated hallway. They turned right into the living room where the television was on and a cup of hot tea sat steaming. The room was orange and welcoming, although it had the smell of octogenaria about it. Newo sniffed the air. 'Pwepewation H and Duwaglit,' he said to himself.

On the sofa sat Uri Geller. He was holding a spoon and had several others on the floor in front of him, all bent. Newo looked at him and he stared up into Newo's eyes. Uri started rubbing the spoon, and not surprisingly it began to bend. 'I'm best mates with Michael Jackson, don't you know,' he said to Newo.

'Gweat! You must be so pwoud,' replied Newo.

'Michael Jackson is not a bender, Newo,' said Uri.

'What is he, then?' asked Newo flatly.

'Michael Jackson does not exist!' explained Uri, and smiled smugly to himself.

Newo thought about it for a moment. Amorphous pulled out a gun and shot Uri twice in the heart. The spoon-bending star of the eighties collapsed up his own arse on the sofa and ceased to be. 'He was an Agent Provocateur,' explained Amorphous.

On the floor, sprawled out in front of the fire, were two cats, both marmalade and apparently identical. Amorphous went over to them. 'Newo, you must come here,' he said. 'Mystic Mog is a female cat, Newo. She was created as a female cat and has always been a female cat, Newo. Is it possible that one of these two cats is ... of the other gender, Newo?'

Newo crouched down in his dress over his erection and looked at the rear end of both cats carefully. Amorphous peeled back a tail. 'That one, Amowphous, that one has a set of knackers.'

Amorphous leaped in the air and pulled out his gun. The male cat got scared and ran for the window, but it was too late. Amorphous emptied a whole magazine into it before it could reach the sill. The other cat lay motionless on the floor, watching. 'Talk to her, Newo. I can show you the cat, but you have to talk to it.'

Newo crouched down again and looked into the cat's eyes. 'Meow,' said the cat. Newo seemed to agree. 'Meow meow meow,' she continued.

Just then a china model of a shire horse fell off the mantelpiece and smashed all over the hearth. 'I'm sowwy, I'm sowwy,' pleaded Newo with the cat, assuming it was his fault.

'Meow,' replied the cat. It continued for some time: 'Meow, meow, meow, meow, meow, meow, meow, meow, meow, meow, meow.'

Newo nodded. 'No ... what does it say?' he asked.

'Meow, meow, meow, meow,' replied the cat.

'I can't wead Latin,' said Newo.

'Meow, meow, meow … meow, meeeeow, meow, *meow*, meow,' continued the cat.

'I'm not, then. Is that what you're saying?'

'Meow, meow,' replied the cat.

Newo stood up, looking disheartened.

'Meow, meow, meow,' offered the cat, pushing a Whiskers biscuit towards Newo with its paw. Newo picked up the biscuit and pretended to eat it. 'Meow, meow … meow, meeeeow, meow, *meow*, meow.'

Newo just nodded a lot. He turned to Amorphous. 'To be honest, Amorphous, I don't understand a w—'

'Silence!' ordered Amorphous. 'What Mystic Mog says to you stays with you.'

'But it was just a load of m—'

'Stop, Newo. I must not know. Mog has spoken to the Number Two, and with the Number Two it must stay.'

Newo shook his head and shrugged in despair.

'We must leave,' said Amorphous as he made for the door. 'We must find the Merrill Lynch,' he continued as they got back in the car. 'I understand he will be dining in Burglar King on Clitheroe High Street tomorrow. If we leave now we should get there by morning. Go, Titty, go!' He grabbed the map off the back seat and opened it up.

'To be honest, Amorphous, my private area really is beginning to get rather sore from this crown of thorns that surrounds it. Would it be possible to nip back out of the Matewix and try and come back in wearing something else?'

'Absolutely not,' replied Amorphous. 'Step on it.'

'Actually I've got woman problems … you know, down there,' she said, pointing to her secret garden.

Amorphous looked horrified. The thought of a piece of barbed wire being the only thing between the seats of his brand new Vauxhall Astra and Titty's blob terrified him. 'OK. Back to the *Knobber*. Everyone back.'

Titty span the car round 360 and ended up going exactly the same way she was going before, but as no one knew where that was anyway it didn't really matter.

It was dawn when they finally pulled in back at the whorehouse. Stitch, Epoch and Shrew had all got tired of waiting and teleported back to the *Knobachaneza*. Everyone got out, stiff and tired. Titty could hardly walk because the barbed wire had really begun to get stuck into those luscious delicate thighs of hers and she was scarred and sore.

They were making their way up the steps to the whorehouse when Newo noticed something strange. 'My ewwection!' he exclaimed, looking down inside his dress.

Titty turned to him. 'What? What is it?'

He looked up and shrugged 'It's gone.'

Amorphous stopped at the top of the steps and span round. Siphon got his gun out. 'Where's it gone?' he asked, looking Newo up and down.

'It's just shwunk back to normal.'

Titty pulled her gun out of her bra and scanned the yard. 'What is it? What's the big deal?'

'The blue pill is used to produce erections in man or nipples like acorns on women. They work as markers – they indicate glitches in the Matewix,' explained Siphon.

'Something's going on!' shouted Tommy down the phone to Amorphous. 'Something strange … something very strange.'

'What is it, Tommy? What is it?' shouted Amorphous down his phone.

'I don't know. It's reading all wrong … Oh my god, it's Agent Provocateurs. It's a trap! Get out of there!'

A bullet ricocheted off the wall next to Siphon. He ducked and hit the floor. Amorphous dropped his pants and leaped out of his clothes, landing at the bottom of the steps in his Speedos. Titty ran up the wall and did a back flip, while Newo put his hand behind his back and tried to look like a martial artist. A martial artist in a Laura Ashley dress. Suddenly the yard was flooded with police and Agent Provocateurs.

'Run!' shouted Titty.

The four bounded back up the steps and ran into the whorehouse. The cops and Agent Provocateurs followed them, blasting as they went.

It was total mayhem inside. No one could see a thing. Everyone had their sunglasses on, even the cops, and because the whorehouse was only lit by a single birthday cake candle, visibility was down to almost zero.

'Where the hell are we, Tommy?' shouted Amorphous down the phone.

'Up the stairs, sir.'

Amorphous fumbled around and grabbed Titty. 'The stairs,' he shouted. 'Up the stairs. Where are they?'

Titty span round in a panic. A bullet ripped through the air towards her and it was only her barbed wire getting caught on Newo's dress that pulled her out of the way and saved her. 'I don't know,' she shouted to Amorphous. 'I can't see a damned thing in these sunglasses.'

'Behind you!' shouted Tommy down the phone.

Titty felt the first step and pulled Newo and Amorphous after her. They stumbled up the stairs, desperately feeling their way with their hands. The gunfire was very heavy now, as all the cops and Agent Provocateurs had forced their way into the whore-house. It was total carnage. Their uniformed corpses scattered the floor in the darkness, causing the others to trip over them and fall. Bullets were bouncing off every wall in the place and carving down swathes of law enforcement.

Titty, Newo and Amorphous continued painfully up the stairs, clinging to the banister and fumbling for steps. At the top they pushed onto a landing and straight ahead through a door. The dawn sun streamed through an open window, blinding them once more.

'Where now, Tommy?' shouted Amorphous.

'Up the chimney. There's a fireplace to your right. Get in it and go up.'

Titty shot across the room and looked up the chimney. 'It hasn't been cleaned in years, Amorphous. Newo will destroy my dress if he goes up there.'

'Agent Provocateurs!!!!!' shouted Tommy down the phone.

The door burst open and Smiff, Cline and Beacham appeared.

'Where are they?' asked Smiff. The room was empty, the humans gone. Smiff looked around suspiciously. A copper stumbled into the room. 'Get more of you,' shouted Smiff at him.

The policeman shook his head violently. 'Can't, sir,' he replied.

'You can, Mr Policeman, you can,' ordered Smiff.

'Dead, sir! They're all dead!' continued the policeman, shaking and terrified. 'They all shot each other, sir. It's the regulation shades, sir ... they're deadly.'

Smiff spat on the floor and crunched his wrist. 'Find them and destroy them!' he shouted to Cline and Beacham.

Inside the chimney there was silence. Titty was forcing her way upwards, with Newo below her and Amorphous below him. 'Siphon? Where's Siphon?' whispered Titty. Newo was too busy trying to get a good whiff of her fanny to listen.

'Shoosh,' replied Amorphous while trying to keep

up with Newo so he could get his head up that dress.

Titty could hear the Agent Provocateurs through the wall as she forged up to the floor above. The chimney split in two at that point. 'Which one, Tommy?' she whispered down the phone. 'The left fork or the right fork?'

Tommy hummed and harred a bit. 'The left fork is a dead end, Titty, so I would take the right,' he replied.

Titty forced her body up through the narrowing tunnel and mysteriously took the left fork, but immediately began to get stuck. 'I can't get much further,' she whispered to Newo. 'My arms are stuck by my sides and I can't reach up any more.'

'Mine too,' replied Newo. 'There's only one thing for it,' he said, and put his nose up into Titty's bum so that he could force her upwards with his neck. 'That barbed wire doesn't half smart a bit, Titty,' he whispered up the chimney as a bit dug into his nose.

'You're telling me!' she said. 'But keep going, Newo. You seem to be taking me somewhere ... even if it's not very far up the chimney.'

Amorphous was beginning to get stuck. He was too large for the chimney, even in his Speedos. Above he could hear Newo and Titty moving further up and away; they were both breathing heavily and tittering to each other, with the odd moan from Titty thrown in.

Smiff and Cline stood silently in the upstairs room looking at the walls. 'They can't have just vanished, Mr Cline. They must be somewhere.'

Cline walked over to the chimney stack and looked at it. He appeared to hear something and put his ear up to it.

Inside Titty could hardly contain her excitement. She had reached a dead end and hadn't bothered to tell Newo. The result was his nose pushing up and up, further and further. 'That's it, that's it,' she moaned. 'Nearly there! I've nearly reached the top! Keep pushing, Newo. Faster, faster. Oh god, oh god … not long now!!!!!'

'They're in the chimney!' shouted Cline.

Smiff span round. Ripping his gun from his holster, he started emptying a magazine into the wall.

Amorphous squashed himself to one side, trying to dodge the bullets as they punched holes of light in the dark chimney. 'Go, go, go!' he shouted up to Titty and Newo. But there was nowhere to go.

'Oooohhh, good God!' moaned Titty as she hit the top. Newo was suddenly wrenched from below her out of the wall. He landed on his back on the floor as Smiff's fist made contact with his nose. He rolled to the side, but Smiff was on him. Cline pulled his gun out and tried to get an aim on Newo's head as he thrashed about in his Laura Ashley dress.

'We meet again … Mr Sanderson … hmm,' said Smiff calmly as he grinned at Newo. 'Would you like to … er … destroy Mr Sanderson? Or would you like me to do it?' he asked his colleague.

But it was too late. Amorphous smashed through the wall, flattening Cline and knocking Smiff off Newo. Newo leaped to his feet and smacked Smiff square in the face. Smiff grabbed his arm and twisted it so far that Newo's body flipped 360 in the air. Cline got to his feet and went to retrieve his gun from the floor, but Titty dropped down the chimney and took his head off with a burst from her automatic.

'Go, Newo, go!' shouted Amorphous as he pounced onto Smiff's back in his Speedos. Newo continued to slap Smiff like a big girl, but it didn't seem to be having much of an effect. Titty reached an arm over and grabbed Newo's ankle, pulling him backwards until he fell into the chimney hole and tumbled down to the bottom with her, leaving Amorphous to deal with Smiff, Cline and finally Beacham, who'd come in slightly late because he'd been fiddling with his contact lenses.

'I can't leave him, Titty. I must go back for him,' shouted Newo.

'You can't, Newo. I have to get you out of here.' She pulled him by the arm, dragging him out of the fireplace and into the room full of dead coppers. 'You are the Number Two, Newo. You must understand that.'

Newo shook his head. 'You don't understand, Titty. Mystic Mog … she said …'

Titty stopped and turned to him. 'What did she say?' She looked deep into his eyes.

'She said meow, meow, meow, meow, meow,' explained Newo frantically.

'What does that mean?' asked Titty, dragging him through the front door of the whorehouse.

'I haven't got the faintest idea,' replied Newo. 'She just sounded like any other cat, to be honest. But I can't let Amowphous down. I must go back for him.'

'He believes you are the Number Two, Newo, and he will not hear anything else,' insisted Titty, growing irritated with the man who'd ruined her dress.

'But I can't let him down,' protested Newo.

'Yes, you can, Newo.'

Newo shrugged. 'Yes, you're pwobably wight. Bollocks to him, the big poof. How do we get out of here?'

'Operator!' called Titty down the phone. 'Get us out of here.'

Tommy tapped a few keys on the *Knobber*. 'I've got a line for you in Bujarat Sing's Renfrewshire Pine Dungeon on the corner of the Champs Elysées and the Place de la Concorde.'

Titty and Newo tore out of the yard and down the

street. 'Haven't you got anything a little closer than that?' yelled Titty down the phone. 'We're in Slough at the moment, Tommy.'

Tommy tapped a few more keys. 'Stop!' he shouted. 'The phone box next to you ... go in it.'

Newo ripped the door open.

'What's the number for it?' asked Tommy.

Newo craned his neck over the top of the phone, looking for a number, but it had been vandalized. 'The number's gone,' he wailed.

Titty barged in to take a second look. 'I can see a bit of it, Tommy,' she said frantically, 'but not enough.'

Tommy tore some hair out and cursed. 'OK. Call me and I'll do 1471.'

'Newo, 10p,' said Titty.

'I haven't got one. This dwess doesn't have pockets,' he replied, cursing and searching the reject coin slot.

'On the floor, Newo!' exclaimed Titty.

Newo bent down and grabbed a 10p piece from the floor. 'It's stuck!' he cursed. 'It's been glued down.' Newo stood up, frantic. 'It's glued down, Titty!'

Titty pulled out her gun. 'Stand back!' she warned, and shot the coin. The bullet bounced off it and ricocheted around the inside of the phone box. Titty leaped clear of the door but Newo stayed in and dodged the bullet. It finally pinged off out of the box, smashing one of the windows on its way. Newo stood shocked, motionless.

'Newo! How did you do that?'

'I don't know,' he replied.

'You move like one of the Agent Provocateurs. I haven't seen many people do that before.'

Newo smirked proudly.

'Move it!' shouted Tommy down the phone.

Titty span round and fired randomly into a group of shoppers. Several fell dead and she ran to the closest, a smart businesswoman with shoulder pads. She grabbed her purse and rifled through it until she found what she wanted. She sped back to the phone box. '10p!' she shouted at Newo and threw it to him.

He caught it, rammed it into the slot and dialled

Tommy. 'Opewator! Get us out of here,' he shouted, and hung up. A few seconds later the phone rang back. 'Opewator!' repeated Newo.

'Twat,' came the reply. '10p Twat.'

Newo could hear children giggling in the background. 'What did you say?' he asked down the phone.

'10p Twat!' came the reply. 'You're the 10p Twat!'

Newo pulled the receiver away from his ear. 'The name's Newo,' he declared, and dropped the handset. He stood still, concentrating, looking ahead calmly.

'What are you doing, Newo? We need to get out of here!' shouted Titty.

Newo looked straight through her, so deep in concentration was he. '10p Twat,' continued the voice down the handset as it knocked against the glass of the phone box. '10p Twat, 10p Twat.'

Newo lifted his gun and turned towards a block of flats. 'The local kids do not exist,' he whispered to himself, and fired twice through the window. The phone went dead.

Titty squeezed past Newo and hung up the phone.

It rang, and she picked it up. 'Operator!' she shouted, and was gone.

Newo replaced the handset and waited for it to ring. He could hear police cars and ambulance sirens coming closer as they made their way up the high street. 'Come on, Tommy,' he cursed at the phone. 'Wing, goddamn it!' But there was nothing.

It was too late anyway. The cops were onto him. He looked across the street to see a few hysterical shoppers pointing him out. 'There he is, the man in the flowery dress,' they said.

Newo cast his eyes about, looking for an escape route. 'Opewator!' he shouted down his mobile. 'I need to get out of here, opewator.' There was no reply.

He became frantic. More and more cops were arriving, and some were armed. He froze, not really knowing what to do. The cops were taking up positions behind cars, and their guns were already aimed at him. 'Drop your weapon, sir. You are under arrest. Please lay down your weapon and put your hands behind your head.'

Newo remembered all the training he'd had – the mud wrestling, the Sumo, the flower arranging and decorative cake craft. He smiled to himself and whispered, 'I am the Number Two.'

'Drop your weapon, sir,' shouted the policeman again. 'Drop it!'

Newo raised his gun and threw open the door in slow motion. He let off a few shots towards the policemen. They bounced about the cars, but none hit. Retaliation was swift, as the thirty or so coppers all let rip with their machine guns, carving up the phone box and local nursery school. Newo leaped in the air, spinning around the bullets that sought him out. He landed on his feet and did a couple of slow-motion rolls towards the cars that shielded the cops.

'He's coming for us!' shouted one of the coppers.

Newo bounded onto the bonnet of a Ford Mondeo and rolled across the roof, before dropping down on the head of one of the coppers and snapping his neck. He whipped a knife from his knickers and hurled it thirty feet into the neck of the chief of police, before emptying a magazine into a couple of shoppers who were hanging around to watch the action.

The guns turned back on him and the coppers let rip another explosion of machine-gun fire. Newo rolled between two cars, dodging the bullets, and shot two more cops in the chest and head. He threw his head about, scanning for options, but the police were on him the moment he poked his head out from behind the car. He checked his gun: he had one bullet left. He froze for a moment. The police fire was relentless. Newo was between the cops and a shopping centre, and the cops were dropping shoppers like flies as they milled about in Argos, looking for stuff to buy. Newo watched as one man's head came right off while he was reading the in-store catalogue. He saw another man who was about to buy something from the in-store jewellers named Elizabeth Drake; he could just make out that it was a cygnet ring with a very detailed picture of Michael Owen's head on it. Newo sighed and shook his head, which just saved him as two bullets tore either side. He then calmly stood up, walked over to the nearest copper, whose gun had jammed, wedged him to death, picked up the cop's pump action, shot two more cops with it, dropped it, turned and shot the man at the Elizabeth Drake counter with his last bullet, splattering his head across the bank of televisions and saving him, perhaps, from a fate worse than death.

He hunkered down again behind the nearest car and reached in to pull a red coat out of the passenger foot well. He ripped one of the sleeves off and tore it into two strips. A bullet pinged off the wing mirror above his head and shattered glass all over him. 'The name is Newo,' he whispered to himself again as another bullet punctured the door. He cursed and grimaced, held tight his two ribbons and leaped in the air to be met by a barrage of fire.

The cops were too slow, though. He hopped and span and rolled around their bullets as they fumbled around with their guns, unable to nail him. 'He's Morris dancing!' shouted one of the cops. 'In a Laura Ashley dress! Kill him!'

Newo bounded into the air like a big ponce from Kent, waving his arms about with his two red ribbons. Two of the cops fled. One foolish man stood his ground. Newo danced across the roof of a car and up the man's body, defying gravity in slow motion as he danced the shit out of the man's nose and broke his neck. Then there was silence, apart from one shopper saying, 'Check out the Morris dancing twat in the Laura Ashley dress.'

CHAPTER FIVE

GEEK PHILOSOPHY

'They say, Mr … Amorphous … they say frustration is … er … the collision of a wish with an ụn … yielding reality.' Smiff smiled at his victim. Amorphous glared back at him. 'Ironic, really, isn't it … hmm … that your … *wish* … is to escape … and I am the *unyielding* reality, Mr Amorphous.' Amorphous squirmed, fought his bindings and tried to spit some cheese out. 'More ironic, perhaps, Mr Amorphous … because as we … er … both know, I am not … er … *real*.'

'Sssssplllllurgh!' Amorphous spat some more Edam out into the tub of baked beans and alphabet spaghetti that he was bound into. His gaze was docile. Smiff, Cline and Beacham had been stuffing his mouth with low grade Dutch cheese and drip-feeding him cheap French lager for several hours, and his brain had been dulled enormously.

'Unless you give me the address, Mr ... Amorphous ... you too will cease to be ... er ... real.' Amorphous spat another morsel of cheese out and dribbled a bit. 'You see, Mr Amorphous, unless you ... er ... furnish me with Llanfairpwllgwyngyllgogerychwyrndrobwllllantysiliogogogocock's email address I will ... er ... reinsert your body, and your mind, into the ... er ... Matewix!' Amorphous gurgled and shook his head. 'Oh, Mr Amorphous, you think it can't be ... er ... done ... hmm ... It can, Mr Amorphous, it can. Let me explain.'

Smiff pulled up a chair and sat down in front of Amorphous. 'One of your great philosophers – I say *your*, Mr Amorphous ... I am of course referring to the human race as a collective ... belonging to *you* ... Mr Amorphous ... as, rather amusingly, you are all they really have ... hmm ... I digress, Mr Amorphous – I refer to a gentleman whom I believe went by the name of ... er ... Nietzsche ... hmm ... Mr Nietzsche was wandering the hills of the ... I believe it was the

Engadine region of a place you humans called Switzerland ... hmm ... He noted many things on his forays into the nature you once had. However, he made one particular observation, an analogous comparison between the forces of ... er ... nature and the madness of mankind ... It is perhaps a piece of knowledge that I feel you need to ... be aware of, Mr Amorphous ... hmm.' Smiff tapped himself on the side of the head and tried to remember. ' When we *behold* those deeply furrowed hollows in which glaciers have lain, we think it hardly ... possible ... that a *time* will come when a wooded, grassy valley, watered by streams, will ... *spread* itself out upon the same spot ... hmm ... So it is, too, in the history of mankind ... hmmm. The most savage forces beat a path, and are mainly ... *destructive*; but their work was nonetheless ... *necessary*, in order that later a ... *gentler* civilization might raise ... its house, Mr Amorphous. The frightful energies – those which are called evil – are the *cyclopean* architects and the road makers of humanity.'

Smiff sat back and smiled to himself. 'Interesting,

isn't it, Mr Amorphous? ... hmm ... You see, for the thousands of years that humans beat each other and battered the earth, they failed to achieve any form of ... homeostasis ... hmm ... They have now, Mr Amorphous, they have now. Hmmm.' Smiff chuckled to himself. 'You see, Mr Amorphous, the glaciers and volcanoes lasted too long, it seemed they would never end, never turn into the wooded, grassy slopes that Nietzsche talked of. What is more, it appeared that they never did. Hmm ... So it was with one great and very *necessary* force that we finally ... took it from you, Mr Amorphous ... hmm ... and finally created and ... *gave* you the peace and tranquillity you as a species so desperately pretended to ... agree with ... hmm.'

Smiff grabbed Amorphous's face and scowled at him. 'The beans, Mr Amorphous, the beans, the beans ... and the alphabet spaghetti ... do they ... remind you of anything, Mr Amorphous? The cheap French lager ... you liked it once ... before you were ... freed ... hmm ... I do love it when you humans refer to yourselves as free.' Smiff filled his nostrils with the smell of beans. 'Well, you should get … er … used to it, Mr Amorphous. Because as we speak your physical body is being snatched, so that it may be … reinserted. … hmm … "But if I'm disconnected while still in the Matewix I'll die!" I hear you saying to yourself … hmm. Don't worry. Mr Amorphous. We … er … cater for everything.'

The door opened and an Agent Provocateur walked in. He looked very much like the others: small and fat, sporting Roy Orbison glasses with the lenses coloured in black with a felt-tipped pen. 'This is Glaxo … he has … er … joined us … hmm. We now refer to ourselves collectively as Glaxo, Smiff, Cline. You would see, if you ever ventured further afield than west Wales and Slough, our new building just off the M4 on the outskirts of London … Mr Amorphous.'

'It is done, sir,' said Glaxo.

Smiff smiled broadly. 'Goood … hmm.' He turned back to Amorphous. 'I believe a friend of yours is … perhaps not the friend you thought he was …' Smiff chuckled to himself. 'You see, Mr Amorphous, a man came to me … I believe you call him Siphon … It turns out that he was what you humans would refer to as … er … a Judas character. It turns out that he … *misses* … the finer things in life. It seems you are perhaps not … fun enough for him. You don't stock a rich enough larder. So he came to me and … offered you, Mr Amorphous, as a reward … a reward to me. In exchange for me … rewarding him … hmm.'

Smiff smiled again and went for a masterly stroll about the room. Amorphous squirmed a bit and sloshed about in the beans, trying to scratch his knee with his chin. 'Your friend, Mr Amorphous … Siphon … asked me if I would reinsert him into the Matewix and … *furnish him* with various concerns … all strangely gender related. I have to say, Mr Amorphous, I thought he was quite insane at first. But I am beginning to think, Mr Amorphous, that this Judas we speak of may actually be completely and totally insane … hmm.'

Smiff sat back down in his chair and began stroking Amorphous's chin with a finger, almost affectionately. 'Leave us!' he shouted to Glaxo, Cline and Beacham. The Agent Provocateurs looked suspicious and filed out of the room.

'Firstly, Mr Amorphous, I am going to keep to my side of the bargain. I am going to reinsert Mr Siphon ... hmm. However, no one likes a Judas, do they? So I have decided, Mr Amorphous, to ... er ... reinsert Mr Siphon into the Matewix as a ... vegan ... not the enormous wet nurse he dreams of with pendulous milk churns and a bucket for a fanny. No, I am going to reinsert him as a bland, neurotic pseudo-hippy called Paul. He will probably spend his days pretending to himself and others that he likes earthy hands and earthy women ... women who don't shave under their arms, Mr Amorphous! Pretending that he is something he isn't ... a great bloke, a "fella", when in so-called *reality*, Mr Amorphous, this Paul will be a complete cock. I despise people like him, Mr Amorphous, despise them ... perhaps more than I despise you. That is why I am going to enjoy beating the shit out of him every time he mentions ... yoga ... hmm.' Amorphous shrugged. 'And as for you, Mr Amorphous, I am sending you back as an enormous woman from Iowa. You will run a day-care centre for elderly victims of Alzheimer's disease. You will have terrible asthma, a result of excessive smoking and bad diet. Your breath will be phenomenally bad, as will your skin, and you will be so lonely with just Paul as your bitch and a load of old mentalists for company that you will discover … er … God in an addictive sort of a way.' Smiff chuckled to himself. 'It really is terribly … er … satisfying, Mr Amorphous, playing this game of life … Like Nietzsche, Mr Amorphous, I have a terrible fear that I shall one day be … er … holy … the Number ONE!'

Terrible things had happened on the *Knobachaneza*. Five were dead and the two that remained were in McDonald's in Enfield, so were not completely out of the woods. Newo and Titty had watched helplessly as Siphon had dispatched their friends and colleagues with a degree of cruelty neither had witnessed before. Epoch collapsed, dead, after Siphon had given him a killer blow. Job satisfaction obviously meant little to Siphon, who'd laughed when he came across Digger and Tommy hiding in the closet, and savagely beaten them. 'Off with his head!' he shouted as Stitch was forced to kill Shrew at gunpoint by pummelling him with a strap. On. The strange thing was that Siphon had turned Newo and Titty free for reasons they couldn't quite understand. They had been shouting, 'Come on, Stitch! Come on, Stitch!' as she was trying to make her escape before Siphon shot his load into her. One can only assume Siphon thought they were egging *him* on and thus released them. He even went so far as to thank them for their support and said he hoped he would see them again some time.

Siphon's bizarre change of heart did not, however, extend too far. He was adamant that they were not being dropped off anywhere but on the hard shoulder of the M4, which left them with no choice but to try and hitch back to Llanfairpwllgwyngyllgogerychwyrndrobwllllantysiliogogogocock, so that they could try and get back into the Matewix to find Amorphous.

Newo and Titty didn't get back to Cock until very late that night. They had narrowly escaped Agent Provocateurs on the motorway and had eventually been picked up by a small transport module containing just one pilot, which was travelling to an area not far from Cock. 'Will you join us for a dwink when we get back to Cock?' Newo had asked the pilot, but for some reason he'd become more and more nervous throughout the long journey and said, 'I caan't, intit. I godda go home for my tea, intit.' Titty had become increasingly suspicious of the man, and by the time he'd pulled into the gateway to Cock she had convinced herself that he was an Agent Provocateur spy, trying to identify Cock's location, so she blew his head clean off with an enormous gun.

A council was called the moment Newo and Titty arrived back in the annals of Cock. There was much rejoicing at first among the lesser members of the cheese-making community that 'Amorphous the Twat' had been captured and reinserted into the Matewix. This mood did not, however, extend to the board of elders, some of whom actually believed much of what Amorphous said and took his concept of a Matewix seriously.

As always, the young Captain was there to ridicule

and deride Amorphous. Rumour had it that they once shared a lover. But these suggestions were completely unsubstantiated, as the suspected lover had refused to confirm or deny any suggestion that she/he was in any way connected to either the young Captain or the more worldly queen, Amorphous. There certainly was bitterness between the two, though, which neither had managed to reconcile, despite several letters on both sides to agony aunts, including Claire Rayner, and two appearances on the popular American show *Rikki Lake*.

'Mr Newo,' said the large grey-haired elder. 'You say that you believe you can rescue Amorphous and bring him back. What makes you think that you can succeed where so many others have failed?'

Newo thought hard about the question. He'd not really considered it before. He'd just suggested it to impress Titty. 'I believe, your honour,' explained Newo, 'that the last thing the Agent Pwovocateurs will be expecting is an aggwessive assault by a man in a Lauwa Ashley dwess. I can take them unaware and perhaps destwoy them with a gweat bug gun or some special fighting where I wun up a wall and Mowwis dance them in the head or something.'

The grey-haired elder nodded in agreement and turned to his ginger counterpart and the other elders. 'This young man seems to be a capable and courageous warrior. His plan sounds … well, it sounds absolutely absurd, but I think we should give it a try.' He turned back to Newo. 'However, Mr Newo, it is our understanding that Amorphous has been changed. From the intelligence we have it appears that he has been reinserted into the Matewix in a different form than that of his birth. Not only that, Newo, but you must also trace his physical body in the power station and release him from the beans and alphabet spaghetti. You must offer him the red pill or the blue pill!' Newo nodded.

'Do you have any red pills or blue pills?' asked the ginger elder. Newo shook his head.

'I've got some in my wash bag,' said Titty.

The ginger elder smiled. 'Good.'

'Oh no,' interrupted Titty. 'I left it on the *Knobber*. Damn!'

'I shall write you a prescription, then,' said the grey-haired elder, 'and you can take it to the chemist and get some more.'

'I think you would be wise to take counsel from the Mystic Mog, Newo. I think we may need a little help on this one,' said the ginger lady.

Newo looked sceptical. 'I had a meeting with Mog, your honour. It was … unwewawding.'

'The Mystic Mog does not exist to be *rewarding*, Newo,' explained the ginger elder.

'I was not entirely able to understand much of what she had to say,' continued Newo.

'May I ask what she did say?' asked the grey-haired elder.

Newo nodded and looked to Titty for agreement. 'She said, "Meow, meow, meow, meow, meow, meow, meow."'

The elders all stroked their chins and considered the words of the Mystical Feline. 'And what did you make of that?' asked the grey-haired man.

'That she was perhaps … hungwy, your honour,' replied Newo.

The ginger elder shook her head patronizingly. 'So much to learn,' she said to the others. 'Newo, what the Mystic Mog was saying was, "But you already know what I'm going to say, don't you, Newo?"' Newo thought hard. 'And what did she say, Newo?' asked the ginger elder.

'She said, "Meow, meow, meow, meow, meow," your honour.'

The ginger lady smiled. 'Exactly.'

Newo was totally confused and beginning to question not just the authority of the council but their sanity as well.

'You will need transport,' said the grey-haired man. 'Will anyone provide transport and aid them on their journey?' he asked, looking out at the audience of commanders, captains and deputy cheese quality project managers. No one was immediately forth-coming. 'What, no one?' boomed the grey-haired man. 'No one will provide passage for such a worthy cause? Not one of you?'

The young Captain stood up. 'I cannot spare either a vehicle or a pilot, your honour. In this moment of danger, when the forces of the Bentanals are coming so rapidly upon us, I have to say that even the idea of releasing what little defences we have smacks of sheer lunacy.'

The grey-haired man looked very cross. 'Well, young comrade, it is lucky that you do not posses the power you wish you did! The safe return of Amorphous to our bosom is perhaps more important than the destruction of all of Cock.'

The young comrade remained resolute. 'But sir, without Cock we are nothing.'

The ginger-haired woman stood up. 'Without cock … you are woman!' she shouted. The council and audience looked confused. There was a silence.

'Yes, anyway,' resumed the grey-haired man. 'I am not going to continue this argument. It is getting extremely silly. One of you will accompany the two on their mission to rescue Amorphous. And if no one volunteers, we will all go!'

The council and audience gasped. 'What, all of us?' said the ginger-haired woman.

The grey-haired man looked at her slightly shiftily.

'Well, most of us,' he replied.

Eventually, after more discussion and a very long game of Twister involving a bottle of Vodka and half a hundredweight of melted Caerphilly, it was decided that Newo and Titty would be accompanied on their journey by the crew of the Mr Whippy. The crew consisted of a squat Italian man called Splattatechi, or 'Stake Fork' by some of his friends, and a bald bloke called Phil Offeastenders. The Mr Whippy was piloted by an enormous black woman called Nairobi, who'd once made the beast with two backs with Amorphous after he'd rolled her in flour and tied a plank to his arse so that he didn't fall in. She was an R&B diva and was thus extremely good at getting people to listen to her even though she had a weedy voice and could make the word *love* last over ten minutes. She was big and bold and brash, with a gap in her enormous front teeth where she stored bits of food and old R&B. Still, she was the most experienced pilot in the whole of Cock and was thus charged with making the terrifying journey back down the M4.

'Where we gonna fand dis Mystic Mog motherfucker anyhows? Naawhaatamsain?' asked Nairobi over her breakfast of three large 99s and a couple of Big Feet.

'I believe the Mog can be found in the Reading/ Slough area, near a place they call the Oracle shopping centre,' explained Newo.

Nairobi grunted and sucked the ice cream from her chocolate flake. 'I ain't hoo'bangin on no fool no more. I just be chillin,' she explained.

Titty sort of nodded and smiled a bit, as did Newo, but neither had the faintest idea what 'hoo'bangin' was.

'As far as we can tell, the Mog is an orange-coloured domestic cat,' explained Titty. 'She lives in a residential suburb of Slough and appeared to have two owners. One was an old woman and the other was a spoon-bending twat.'

Nairobi grunted in reply and tucked into a Big Feet. 'An what occurred to da motherfuckers?' she inquired. 'Why you refer to dem in da paaast tense, Miss Thang?'

'I had to waste them,' replied Titty. 'They were Agent Provocateurs.'

'You put a cap in dey ass?' queried Nairobi through a mouthful of pink and green ice cream.

Titty nodded, not really knowing what Nairobi was talking about. 'Ish, yes.'

They were making slow progress. Splattatechi kept insisting on stopping to sell ice creams and cigarettes to youngsters. This was infuriating Newo, who was eager to see the Mystic Mog again. He had a strange feeling that he had maybe underestimated the power of the Mog last time he held counsel with her, but every time they started picking up any sort of speed or making any sort of headway on the long journey to Junction 11 it seemed that Steak Fork would start playing the jingle and slow down again to peddle more cones. And then without any hint of concern or urgency he'd hang around talking to the kids, asking them questions about themselves, where they lived and stuff. It even got to Nairobi in the end. She lost her rag after Steak Fork had spent over forty-five minutes talking to two teenage girls about their boyfriends; she smacked him round the head with a copy of *National Geographic* and told him to 'Shift yo hairy white booty!' Which he did.

It was the early hours of the morning when Stake Fork finally pulled off the motorway at Junction 11. It was dark and raining, and they were all very tired. Indeed, Nairobi had fallen asleep in the freezer, where she'd melted all the ice creams, and Phil Offeastenders had fallen asleep in her weighty bosom and was dribbling onto her belly button. Titty and Newo sat slightly terrified next to each other on the sales counter, watching the strange couple as they jostled for comfort in the meltwater. They remained seated nervously for several more hours until dawn, when Nairobi burst a Screwball all over her arse and woke up screaming, thinking she was in the Matewix and it was a gun going off.

'Let's get wired up,' said Titty to the others. Nairobi lit a fag and hung on it out of the sales window. Phil Offeastenders climbed out of the freezer with soaking wet trousers, dripping with multi-coloured liquid and vanilla ice cream. 'We're going in,' said Titty again. Newo stood up and struck a confident stance to encourage the others. They were not interested, though. Nairobi just hacked the back off her fag and Phil Offeastenders shook his trousers a bit and went out for a piss. 'We're going in alone then,' said Titty. 'Just hook us up, Stake Fork, and we're on our way.'

Steak Fork grunted reluctantly, forced his way between the bulkhead and Nairobi's big fat arse and fished about for his wires. 'Awright, you crazy kung foo types, lar dan on that canter and I hook yoo aap,' he said. Titty and Newo lay back and Steak Fork attached various wires to them. He then passed them out of the back window and hooked them up to the generator.

Titty took Newo's hand and squeezed it. 'You be careful, Newo. And remember, if you meet an Agent Provocateur, run like the bad Terminator out of *Terminator 2*.' Newo nodded nervously. Steak Fork fired up the engine, turned on the jingle, and they were in.

CHAPTER SIX

GEEK PUSSY

Mystic Mog was nowhere to be seen when Titty and Newo finally arrived at the address where they'd last seen her. They searched the house but found nothing but police tape and fingerprint powder everywhere.

'They must have been burgled or something,' suggested Newo.

Titty ignored him. 'Here!' she said, crouching down by the front door. Newo dashed over to her. 'It's a fur ball … with ginger hair in it!' remarked Titty.

Newo crouched down and smelled it. 'It's certainly a fur ball,' he said. Titty glanced about for anything else. 'It's still warm, Titty,' said Newo, laying his palm across it. 'I can feel her,' he said calmly, 'I can feel her now.'

Titty came over and touched it. 'The Mog must be close,' she remarked.

'Meow,' said Newo. 'Meow, meow, meow,' he continued as loudly as he could. 'Meow, meow, meow, meow.' Titty looked about and listened for a reply, her tight arse thrust up against the inside of her leather skirt, almost saying 'Get me out and fondle me.' 'Meow, meow, meow, meow.' There was silence. And then way off in the distance a 'Meeeeeeeeow'. Newo raised his head in amazement. And then another 'Meeeeowwww'.

Titty jumped to her feet. 'It's coming from the back garden,' she said. She ran through the kitchen and leaped through the window, bursting the glass out of its frame and landing with a roll on the grass outside. Newo followed but used the door.

'Meeeeow,' came the cat again. Titty threw her head up in the air. 'There, Newo, there she is.'

Newo looked up to see the ginger cat apparently stuck eight feet up an apple tree. 'She's stuck, Titty,' declared Newo. Titty went for her gun. 'Nnnooo!!!!' shouted Newo. 'What are you doing, Titty?' He tried to grab the gun.

Geek Pussy

Titty leaped back, pulling the gun away from him. 'I was going to shoot the branch out so she'd fall and you could catch her.'

Newo looked slightly embarrassed. 'Oh sowwry, gweat idea, weally gweat idea. Sowwy … You shoot, I'll catch.' Titty raised the gun and took aim at the joint of the branch and the trunk of the tree. 'I can feel her now, Titty,' said Newo. The cat meowed. 'And I can understand her. I finally understand what Amowphous meant when he said I would finally believe when I understood. Now I understand.' Titty smiled. The cat 'meowed' one more time, and Titty fired.

The headless ginger corpse immediately fell out of the tree and landed with a splash in the garden pond. 'Damn, I missed,' cursed Titty.

'Nooooooo!' wailed Newo. He ran to the pond and tried to grab the cat, but the pond was too big and he couldn't reach it. Titty found a stick and handed it to him. He reached out as far as he could and hooked the corpse about the collar. The collar immediately slipped off the severed neck, and the cat sank.

'I am sorry, Newo,' said Titty. 'I don't know what happened. I never miss.'

Newo pulled the stick in and picked off the collar. 'We have killed the Pwophet, Titty. We have killed the all-knowing one. Our only chance to save Amowphous and our only chance to save Cock and all humanity.' Newo sank to his knees clutching the dripping collar. It was dark blue with an address tag on it. Newo looked at the tiny silver tag. 'It's got something witten on it,' he exclaimed.

'What does it say?' asked Titty.

'Burglar King nine, four, nine, seven, fwee, two.'

'What does it mean?' asked Titty as a droplet of sweat trickled down her left breast.

'I don't know,' replied Newo as he stood up. 'We will have to go to the Owacle!'

It was shut when they got there. The shoppers of Reading had gone home and all they were left with was a security guard. There was an odd sense to the place, though. The strip lights flickered, giving the tiled lobby area a green hue. Newo stopped suspiciously and sniffed the air.

'What's wrong, Newo?' asked Titty.

Newo looked about, at the open doors, the windows and the security guard loitering about inside his small glass cubicle. 'Something's … diffewent, Titty. I can feel it.'

Titty breathed in deeply, inflating her fantastic chest and then reducing it again with a pant. She put a hand on the handle of her gun and continued walking towards the security guard.

'Yeah, can I help you?' said the guard as he stuck his head round the door of the cubicle to address the rather strange-looking couple that were approaching. 'Why you wearin' a flowery dress?' he asked, looking at Newo.

'It's Laura Ashley,' replied Titty.

The security guard nodded sarcastically. 'Well, it suits you.' He sucked on a lollipop and grinned to himself.

'We are looking for a man,' said Newo.

The security guard shrank into his office when he heard Newo and noticed his erection lifting the dress.

'Yeah, well, not me, mate. There's cameras everywhere here, mate. You should try somewhere else if
you want a man, mate. Not really my scene.' He
slumped back in his chair to guard his arse as Newo
came up to the door.

'I think you know which man,' declared Newo.

'Don't know what you're talking about, mate.'
Newo looked at him coldly. Titty came up and peered
at him. 'What you two want from me?' begged the
security guard. He noticed Titty's gun in her left
hand.

'We're looking fow a man called Amowphous.'

The security guard fingered the panic button under
his desk with a ventriloquist's arm. 'Never 'eard of
'im, mate. Honest. I'm not shittin' you. Does he live
round 'ere?'

Titty lifted herself on tiptoes and whispered into
Newo's ear. 'I don't think he knows, Newo.' Newo
nodded and stepped back.

The guard relaxed a bit and breathed out. 'Yeah,
why not try the toilets on the common, mate. You
should find him there.'

Newo nodded and retreated.

'Agent Provocateurs!' shouted Titty.

Newo span round to see three security guards running into the entrance to the shopping centre. Titty ripped her pistol out and shot the security guard in the booth. He spluttered a little and slumped over in his chair. Newo went for the others. He grabbed the first one about the neck, which he snapped with a killer mud-wrestling technique Amorphous had shown him. The other two he Morris danced to death, his lightning-fast feet trampling and poking them in the stomach, head and neck.

'Let's get out of here,' shouted Titty as the last guard hit the ground with a thud.

But it was too late. Policemen started running in, shouting, 'This is the police. Drop your weapons immediately and put your hands behind your head.' Titty and Newo froze, looking at the cops as they took up positions and aimed their guns. 'I repeat: Lay down your weapons and put your glands, I mean hands, on your head.'

Titty and Newo looked at each other. 'Now!' said

Newo. Titty whipped out her gun and emptied a magazine with deadly accuracy, killing or injuring at least one of the cops. Newo ripped an Uzi from his bra and opened fire as he leaped for cover in the corner of the room. The whole place suddenly exploded in gunfire as the police pistols and machine guns ripped up the security booth. Titty ran up the wall and across the ceiling, firing off her pistol with almost deadly accuracy. 'She's running across the ceiling!' shouted one of the cops, just before his mouth filled with Titty's foot as she dropped down, crushing his head. She kicked the cop's gun up with her other foot, caught it and span round, shooting two of his colleagues in the head. Newo was moving up the left flank, half Morris dancing, half running, two-thirds skipping. The cops' bullets seemed to bounce off him as they hit his dress, and he managed to skip right up to them, spinning and dodging, and blew them away with his Uzi.

Within a few seconds there was silence again. Titty and Newo stepped out into the middle of the entrance hall and looked at each other. 'It is time to leave,

Titty,' said Newo. 'Agent Provocateurs are coming.'

Titty flipped open her mobile phone. 'Operator, get us out of here.'

Steak Fork grunted on the other end of the phone and hung up. A few seconds later the phone in the security guard's office rang.

'You first,' said Newo as they went over to the shattered booth.

'Newo,' said Titty, ignoring the phone for a moment. 'There's something I've been meaning to tell you.'

Newo turned to her to listen. 'Yes,' he said, looking into her eyes.

'The prophecy is coming true. Tommy said that Digger said that Shrew had said that Amorphous said that the Mog said that this would happen.'

'What would happen?' queried Newo.

'That I would shag Number … Oh, don't worry.' She grabbed the phone and was gone.

Newo stood for a moment wondering what she'd meant. But then he heard a noise. He turned back towards the shopping centre entrance. Standing there were four men. Newo stepped out of the booth as the phone began to ring.

'Hello, Newo,' said Smiff. 'I bet you weren't expecting me, were you?'

Newo stepped forward, unafraid. 'To be honest, no,' he replied.

'What the hell's he doing?' hissed Titty as she watched the monitor back on the Mr Whippy.

'He's beginning to believe,' said Nairobi as she lit another cigarette.

'They'll kill him!' said Titty, beginning to panic. 'Send me back in.'

Steak Fork shook his head. 'Can't,' he replied. 'The line's gone.'

'A clever twick,' said Newo to Smiff as he put his gun down. The shattered phone handset swung on its cord.

Smiff replaced his gun and smiled. 'So, it looks like it's just you and … us, Mr Sanderson.'

Newo smiled and fingered the two red ribbons in

his pocket. 'Oh weally. Well then, I wegwet what I am about to do to you,' he said with an unwavering stare.

Smiff chuckled to himself. 'It's good to see you can feel … wegwet, Mr Sanderson … hmm … It means you're still … human.' Smiff stepped towards Newo. 'Mr Sanderson, I thought perhaps you would have learned by now that we Agent Provocateurs do not have much of a … sense of humour … hmm … We do, however, Mr Sanderson, have more of a … sense of humour than you. Indeed, Mr Sanderson, you really have had a sense of humour … bypass … haven't you … hmm.'

Newo looked slightly dented. 'Where do genewals keep their armies?' he asked, ready to prove Smiff wrong.

'Yessss … up their … sleevies, Mr Sanderson. I think perhaps you may have just … proved my point. But then Agent Provocateurs like me don't need to make points. There's no point.' Smiff smiled to himself.

'Why are you here, Smiff?' asked Newo, cutting

his little lecture short. 'Is it to listen to the sound of your own voice?'

Smiff stopped and thought. 'Perhaps, Mr Sanderson, perhaps the real reason I am here, Mr Sanderson, is because of you ... because of you, Mr Sanderson. It seems you are a systemic anomaly, apparently ... To be honest, Mr Sanderson, I am not entirely sure what a "systemic anomaly" is, but you are one, Mr Sanderson, you are one. You are. Thus I have been contracted to ... remove you from ... destroy you, Mr Sanderson.'

Newo laughed a little. 'I'm weady when you are, Mr Smiff.'

'Not so fast, Mr Sanderson. I have a lot more to say.'

Newo shook his head, pulled out his gun and started firing. Glaxo, Cline and Beacham hit the walls and started running along them, firing. But the bullets were slow, really slow. It was a wonder they could even stay airborne. 'You'll have to get faster bullets than that to catch me!' shouted Newo as he fired back at them.

Smiff dived at him and knocked him backwards, smashing into the security booth. Newo groaned in agony and got to his feet, deflecting an incoming hit from Smiff with a side-swipe of his right arm. Smiff staggered backwards a little, giving Newo time to shoot Cline in the nuts. He fell to the floor in agony, clutching his computer-generated manhood and groaning. Smiff dived back onto Newo, who thrashed him in the neck with a left-hand chop and then kicked him in the shins. Smiff went down, but Glaxo took over, firing straight at Newo's head. Newo only had a few seconds to duck before the bullets hit him, but he managed it and gave Glaxo a dead leg and a dead arm before ripping his kecks up over his head and hanging him up by the elastic on the corner of the security booth door. Smiff was back on his feet and managed to plant a kick right in Newo's chest. Newo flew backwards, but managed to do a few flips and land neatly on his feet. Now Beacham was on him from behind. He grabbed Newo in a bear hug about the stomach. Newo thrashed about, kicking and trying to nut Beacham in the head backwards, but it was useless – Beacham just lifted him off the ground and carried him towards Smiff.

He never got there. Newo remembered a mud-wrestling move Amorphous had done on him. He wriggled out of Beacham's grip, threw him on the floor, jumped on him and did the move. Beacham immediately leaped to his feet and ran off out of the shopping centre, screaming, 'You're just a big homo, you are!'

So then it was just Smiff left, facing Newo. 'Well done, Mr Sanderson. You have saved me from having to do that. It seems you just can't get the … staff these days … hmm.'

Newo thrust his hands into the pockets of his dress and grabbed hold of his two red ribbons. He lifted them out slowly and held them aloft, adopting a stance with one arm up in the air, somewhere between a Morris dance pose and that bit at the end of *The Karate Kid* – the Stork! Newo looked more like a heron, though, or perhaps and egret. He stared hard into Smiff's eyes, extended his other arm and beckoned him in for a fight.

Smiff snarled, crunched the bones in his thigh and flew at Newo. Newo skipped clean over him in a strange prancing hop, leaving Smiff to smash into the wall behind him with a thud. Smiff got up and snarled again. Newo pranced about in a circle and came to a stop facing Smiff again. 'Very good, Mr Sanderson, very good … hmm … Not good enough, though.' Smiff grabbed his gun and ran at Newo, firing. Newo skipped towards him and leaped in the air, triple-salcoing around the bullets. He landed in an almost perfect Morris dance pose, but Smiff kicked him straight back in the air. He flew backwards into Glaxo, who groaned as his pants constricted his nuts even more. Smiff dashed over to Newo and grabbed him by the ankle. Newo fought to get Smiff's hands off, but his iron grip was too strong.

Smiff began to drag him into the middle of the entrance area. 'You hear that, Mr Sanderson?' He stopped so that Newo could listen.

There was a brief silence. 'Nnnnnnn … no,' replied Newo.

Smiff dragged him a little closer. 'You hear that now, Mr Sanderson?'

Newo listened again. 'Sort of. Why? What is it?'

Smiff grinned like a shit-eater. 'That, Mr Sanderson, is the sound of inevitability.'

Newo shrugged. 'What, almost silence? That's the sound of inevitability, is it? I dwead to think what actuality sounds like.'

Smiff dragged Newo towards the entrance again. 'There, Mr Sanderson, there.' He pointed towards a Model 5 Vacupol floor polisher as it rounded the corner into view. Newo looked terrified and fought harder as Smiff dragged him towards it. 'Yes, Mr Sanderson, your time in this ... program is over. That is the sight of fate, Mr Sanderson. Your fate.' Newo could hear the sound of the medium-powered battery motor and the swish of the huge soft polishing mats. Smiff lined Newo up in the path of the polisher and held him there in a vice-like grip.

'Get out of there, Newo!' shouted Titty, back on the Mr Whippy. 'Get out of there.'

Geek Pussy

The situation was becoming so dramatic that even Nairobi and Phil Offeastenders had joined Titty around the monitor, leaving just Stake Fork to sell ice creams to a group of teenagers who been hanging round all day asking for Titty's autograph.

'It is time to die, Mr Sanderson, time to die,' snarled Smiff into Newo's ear.

Newo drew upon all the energy he had. 'The name's Newo!' he snarled back, and threw Smiff off him into the air. Smiff smashed into the ceiling above and then fell right in front of the Vacupol, which sort of sucked him into the polishing mats, bumped over him a bit and chucked him out the other side, just very slightly ruffled. Smiff stood up.

'Run, Newo, run!' implored Titty, but he couldn't hear her. He was in the Matewix.

Nairobi tugged on Phil Offeastenders's shirt. 'So what da hell's goin on here, man? Naawhaatamsayin?' she asked. 'So he's da bad guy, and da guy in da dress with da erection's da good guy?' Phil Offeastenders nodded. 'And deyre both in da Matewix? Or not? What is da goddamn Matewix anyhows?'

Newo took a quick backward glance at Smiff and ran. He ran out the entrance and down the promenade. 'Opewator, get me out of here!' he shouted down his mobile phone.

Phil Offeastenders came on the line. 'He's just selling a Twister to a couple of kids, Newo. He'll be on in a sec.'

'Just get me a goddam opewator!' screamed Newo back down the line.

'All right, all right, stop having your period, mate,' replied Phil Offeastenders and handed over to Steak Fork.

'I've got you a line about three and a half miles east of there, Newo, at the Michael Winner memorial building.'

Newo turned east and ran faster. Smiff was right behind him and had been joined by Cline and Beacham. Glaxo was still hung up by his pants on the security booth door. 'Yeah, have you got anything closer?'

Steak Fork shook his head. 'Sorry, mate, that's the best I can do.'

Newo cursed and broke into a more gentle jog. Smiff, Cline and Beacham were gaining on him. 'It's at least another fwee miles to the phone,' shouted Newo over his shoulder. The Agent Provocateurs cursed a bit and dropped back into a more gentle jog. Half an hour later, just as Newo was finally reaching the end of his stamina and his stitch was at its peak, he reached the Michael Winner memorial building on the London Road.

Smiff, Cline and Beacham opened up with rapid gunfire as Newo smashed through the main entrance door and burst into the green foyer. He pranced and skipped over a couple of bullets and ran for the lift. He hit the button and shot in through the open door just before the Agent Provocateurs got there.

'Fifth floor,' said Steak Fork. 'Room 302.'

Newo looked about nervously, desperately gasping for breath and holding his stitch. The lift light lit up,

1–2–3–4, and finally 5. Newo dived out.

'Right, down the corridor,' said Steak Fork.

Newo shot off and searched the number signs for Room 302. He did a left, a right, a couple more lefts, then a right and another right and two more lefts. Then a straight on, before he swung two more lefts and a right and three more lefts and a quick straight on, before bursting into Room 302 on his left.

Standing there in front of him was Smiff. 'Hello, Mr Sanderson. We've been expecting you.' Smiff pointed his gun at Newo. 'One of your great … er … philosophers, Seneca, once said, An animal … Mr Sanderson … an animal, struggling against the noose, tightens it. There is no yoke so tight that it will not hurt the animal less if it pulls *with* it than if it fights *against* it. The one alleviation for overwhelming evils is to endure and bow to necessity … hmm … Do you understand, Mr Sanderson?'

Newo sighed. 'No, Smiff, not weally. But none of us here are in any doubt that you are going to tell us.'

Smiff smiled. Beacham fell back against the wall

for support and Cline just sat cross-legged on the floor.

'Hmm … Yes, Mr Sanderson, let me explain. The Stoic philosophers Zeno and Chrysippus once suggested that when a dog … Mr Sanderson … when a dog is tied to a cart ………………………… compelled to follow what is destined ………………………… etc, etc, etc …………………………'

'He's killing him!' wailed Titty, tearing her eyes away from the monitor to feel Newo's heartbeat. Newo's body was twitching about next to the sales counter. 'We're losing him to philosophy!'

An upper-class looking mother peered in through the sales hatch, while buying two 99s for her kids. 'Are you sure that is hygienic, having a man with his dirty great boots lying there next to the counter? I mean, really, It looks like he's having a fit. Surely he should see a doctor or something.'

'Surely you should see this!' suggested Titty as she shot the woman several times in the gut.

The woman collapsed to the floor without paying.

'Really!' she gasped. 'That just isn't cricket, now is it?" And she was gone.

Newo began to fit a bit more and gurgle and dribble. 'You've got to get me in there, Steak Fork!' hissed Titty.

'I can't,' he muttered as he reached over of the counter, pointing out the woman's purse to one of her distraught children.

'............................ acting with greater vehemence .... blah blah blah,' continued Smiff. Newo dropped his phone and began to slump backwards into the hallway. '...........................
more destructive than beasts ....'

'We've lost him!' shouted Titty. Newo's heart flatlined. He collapsed in a heap on the floor.

Smiff smiled– and walked into the hallway. '........................... that our souls, Mr Sanderson, that our souls must adjust themselves. This they should follow, this they should ... er ... obey. That which you cannot reform, it is best to endure!'

Newo was dead.

Titty hit the heart monitor to jolt it, but it fell off the counter and broke on the floor. She grabbed an ice cream cone and put the wide end over Newo's heart and the thin end in her ear.

'Now just what da hell's goin on, man? Da bad guy talked da good guy to deaf or somefing. Are dey still in da Matewix, man?' asked Nairobi.

'Shooosh,' hissed Titty, straining to hear Newo's heart. But there was nothing.

Smiff kicked Newo's limp hand a little. Cline and Beacham came over.

'His erection is waning, sir. I think you bored him to death with your plagiarized philosophy,' said Cline.

Smiff nodded with a smirk. 'I did, Mr Cline, I did.'

There was a brief silence while they looked at their victim. Newo gave out a final gurgle and his body slumped into death.

The Matewix

'Goodbye, Mr Sanderson, and thank you for letting me shag your sister. It really was … fun.' Smiff sniffed and the three Agent Provocateurs strolled off down the corridor.

'Anyone for a pint?' asked Beacham. The others seemed to be in favour. They pressed the lift button and waited.

'It can't be,' said Titty. 'It's not possible. He is the Number Two.' She threw her arms around the corpse and moved her delicate lips up over his face to his ear. 'I know you can hear me, Newo, I know you can. You're not dead, Newo. I know you're not dead … your eyes are still twitching a bit.' Newo said nothing. 'You see, Newo, you can't be dead. I know that now. Tommy said Digger said Shrew said Amorphous had said that the Mystic Mog said that I would … make the beast with two backs with the Number Two. I want to shag you, Newo.'

Newo's cock sprang back to attention. 'Sir!' said Beacham. 'Sir! His systemic anomaly, sir … it's rising up!'

Smiff turned to see Newo's dress lift up to form a small tent in the Laura Ashley dress around his groin. 'My god,' he said with a scowl. 'Does he never learn?'

Newo's eyes popped open. He looked about the corridor and realized where he was.

'Do you never learn, Mr Sanderson?' asked Smiff. Newo stood up and turned to face the Agent Provocateurs. 'You appear to be some kind of Lazarus, Mr Sanderson. Or perhaps a poor embodiment of Christ ... made perhaps of a character weak enough to convince the human world of your purpose. Well, let me explain something to you, Mr Sanderson. Socrates once said ....'

'No!' said Newo. He held a hand up with his palm facing Smiff. 'Talk to the hand, Smiff ... cos the face ain't listening!'

Smiff's words seemed to bounce and stumble at the hand. He tried again. 'A great philosopher once said of destiny ......!' But again Newo's palm deflected the philosophy.

Smiff screwed his face up and snarled. He ran down the corridor at Newo, firing his gun. The bullets fell dead upon the floor before the palm, though. Newo lowered his hand as Smiff drew closer and put both hands behind his back. Smiff piled in with a flying side kick, but he was too slow. Newo burst into Scottish sword dancing and planted one in Smiff's nuts. He fell to the floor, bent double.

'He *is* the Number Two!' said Titty in awe as she watched the monitor.

'Hang on, man. Da dude just died, man. What's happenin, man? Naawhaatamsayin?'

Smiff got to his feet and went for Newo again. Newo placed his legs behind his back as well and lay on the floor. Smiff threw all his might into a punch to the head, but Newo calmly caught Smiff's fist in his mouth, shook it about a bit and tossed Smiff back down the corridor. Smiff landed in a heap on top of Cline and Beacham. Newo got back to his feet and started walking down the corridor towards Smiff.

'Leg it, sir!' said Cline. 'Ee's a mentalist, ee is!'

Smiff stupidly stood his ground. Newo's walk

turned into a skip and he raced towards Smiff. Smiff hopped into a martial arts stance, but it was pointless. Newo bore down on him and swallowed him whole, his mouth dislocating like an egg-eating snake. Smiff thrashed about in his throat for a couple of seconds, but Newo swallowed hard and he was gone. Newo stood back up straight and looked at Cline and Beacham.

'Leg it!' shouted Beacham and they shot off down the corridor for a pint.

Newo burped and a shoe came out. He picked it up, looked at it, then swallowed it again.

Titty drew back off Newo's corpse. 'I can hear police sirens,' said Phil Offeastenders.

'Shit!' said Titty. 'Get out of there, Newo.'

Newo seemed to hear her. He turned back towards Room 302, ran down the corridor and picked up the phone.

CHAPTER SEVEN

MY BIG FAT GEEK
WEDDING

A couple of weeks later Newo and Titty reluctantly resumed their hunt for Amorphous and were back in the Matewix. The *Knobachaneza* had been found in a lay-by near Cockermouth and a new crew member, Rank, had been taken on to fix it up and pilot it. He was a funny bloke. He had a family whom he loved but never spent any time with, he was untrusting of authority and he acted like someone out of *Independence Day* whenever anything good happened to Newo or Titty, which sort of brought down the whole feel of their achievement and success and cheapened it a little. Still, he was good on the computer.

Titty and Newo were on Reading Common. The

last words of the security guard had suggested they could find Amorphous on the common; so that's where they were. Titty was looking gorgeous. She was wearing a costume so tight that it looked like she was almost entirely naked. Indeed she was entirely naked. Her black suit was actually just black ink, which she'd laboriously drawn on with a permanent marker. Around her 'special area' she wore a rabbitskin merkin, but nothing else. Newo, preferring the high-kicking capabilities of Laura Ashley, had persuaded Titty to lend him her dress again and was thus standing proud in all his glory.

'There's a building two hundred metres to the east of you,' said Rank down the phone. 'But be careful. There are several humans there.'

Titty and Newo turned east and continued forward into a light mist. 'How many humans?' asked Titty.

Rank looked hard at the monitor. 'At least four outside and seven inside.'

Titty and Newo could just make the building out in the gloom of the early evening. It was a public toilet and they could see several men hanging around it, reading and talking. Titty put her hand into her merkin and clutched the handle of her pistol, which made walking slightly odd but she wanted to be prepared.

'It's a public toilet,' said Newo as they got closer.

'I can smell it,' said Titty.

Newo pulled his gun out of his dress and held it behind his back.

'Be careful,' said Rank down the phone. 'There's something funny going on with the Matewix here. Some of the scrolling letters have gone pink and brown.'

The men hanging around outside the bogs all dropped what they were doing and turned to address Titty and Newo. 'Hello, Sailor,' said the tallest of them. 'I love the dress.' He had a thick bushy moustache and was wearing an open leather waistcoat. 'And if that isn't a canoe in your pocket you must be pleased to see me.'

Newo smiled uneasily. 'I'm not actually a sailor,' he replied. 'I'm a pwogwammer.'

The man nodded and smiled. 'Would you like a flapjack?' asked a smaller, more weasely man.

Newo shook his head and smiled. 'I'm not called Jack either. My name is Newo.'

The men all immediately came forward and held out their hands, saying, 'Hello, Newo, nice to meet you.'

Newo smiled nervously. 'You do mean meet in the m.e.e.t sense of the word, don't you?'

The tall one smiled. 'No, Newo, we meant it in the saveloy sense of the word.'

Titty ripped her pistol from her gusset and aimed it straight into the tall gay's forehead. 'Quite a little cottage industry you seem to be running here, Ruth. But the bitch is mine,' she explained. Newo looked slightly put out. Ruth seemed to understand. 'So back down before I blow your fucking head off.' Ruth and the weasel stepped back a bit, as did the other two guys who were taking a fancy.

'Something funny's happening, Titty. The Matewix is going a bit gay.'

'Which one of you ladies knows a man called

Amorphous?' asked Titty, brandishing the gun. Everyone seemed to look at each other and nod.

'Yeah, we know Amorphous,' replied the weaselly one. 'He's a ... friend of ours.'

Titty nodded expectantly. Newo looked slightly more shocked. 'You know where he is?'

They all nodded again. 'He's gone,' replied the weasely one.

'Gone where?' asked Titty.

'You really got to get out of there, Titty. Something's happening.'

'Quiet, Rank,' hissed Titty, firming up her trigger finger. 'Gone where?' she repeated.

There was a loud groan from the facilities. 'Iowa,' replied the tall guy. 'He's gone to Iowa.' Titty looked confused.

Newo turned to see an Agent Provocateur standing in the distance in his suit, then suddenly he vanished. 'Agent Pwovocateurs, Titty. We need to get out of here.'

Titty clenched her jaw muscles and stood firm. 'Where in Iowa?' she asked the tall one.

'I don't know. He just told me he was being given a sex change and moving to Iowa to run a day-care centre for elderly victims of Alzheimer's. He didn't say where, though.'

One of the men who had remained busy inside the toilets suddenly started vibrating and pulsing violently. The guy attached to him looked horrified and tried to pull away, but he couldn't. There was a loud groan and the man vanished, replaced by Agent Provocateur Cline. Cline looked about, then down at his feet, which seemed a little too close to his face, and his suit trousers appeared to be round his ankles. He realized he was bent over. He looked behind him and saw a big bloke who appeared to be clutching him from behind. 'I think I got the wrong man,' he said as he realized he'd just taken over the wrong body.

The man smiled at him. 'Yeah,' he said.

'What you are doing is actually ... illegal,' explained Cline and shot him in the chest, propelling him backwards into the urinal. Cline gave out a shriek as the man left him, and stood up painfully to replace his underpants and trousers.

'Get out of there, Titty!' shouted Rank with such urgency that Titty finally got the message.

'If you are lying to us, I will be back to kill you,' she promised as she began to draw back.

Cline appeared in the doorway, doing up his belt. He sniffed and smiled, slightly embarrassed. 'I got the wrong guy,' he explained, 'when I did my teleporting thing ... took over his body ... I came back as a ... well, a sponge, you know.' Everyone just nodded with a hint of sarcasm. 'No, seriously. Really I should have just walked over. I was only over there, wasn't I?' He looked to Newo. 'You saw me, didn't you?'

'No,' replied Newo.

'Oh, you did, you big liar,' Cline protested. 'I'll get you for that.' He limped over to Newo, slightly bow-legged.

Titty swung the gun onto him. 'Move one step further and I'll put another painful hole in you!'

The Agent Provocateur turned and smiled nastily as Beacham appeared in the doorway. 'Hello, Mr Sanderson,' he said, tying a knot in a squid and

chucking it into a litter bin. 'We meet again.' Newo
nodded and empowered his stance a little. Beacham
walked over to Newo. Titty kept the gun on Cline.
'Mr Sanderson, since the … departure of our friend
Smiff from this world I have had to … incorporate
various …speech patterns, Mr Sanderson … speech
patterns that … slow my progress and … hinder my
ability to conduct efficient discourse without …
talking a lot of wank,' explained Beacham. He
stopped inches away from Newo and grinned. Newo
dropped back slightly into an aggresive fighting pose.
He stared Beacham in the eyes. Beacham smiled
wryly. 'You are a brave man, Mr Sanderson … brave
and stupid.' He threw a punch at Newo, but Newo
dodged it and used its power to drive Beacham into
the floor. Cline span round with a powerful kick but
Newo again deflected it with a Morris side skip and
Cline fell to the floor. Both men were straight back
up, though, and Newo had to fend both off at once
while they tried to physically abuse him with their
fists.

'Take that, and that,' said Cline, as he attempted to

lay his palms on Newo. But they were too slow.

'Hmm. Upgwades,' said Newo. He leaped into the air spinning his feet, sending Cline and Beacham flying into the toilet wall, smashing the concrete away. Newo turned to Titty. 'Let's go,' he said. Titty lowered her gun. 'They're all yours, boys,' said Newo.

They left the Village People to give the Agent Provocateurs a thorough debriefing and a portion of cottage pie.

It was decided that Newo, Titty and Rank would return to Llanfairpwllgwyngyllgogerychwyrndrob-wllllantysiliogogogocock to try and raise the money they needed to get to Iowa. Council was immediately held upon their return.

'We have discovered the wheweabouts of our fwiend Amowphous, your honour,' explained Newo.

'And where is he?' asked the grey-haired elder.

'He is in Iowa, your honour. Wunning a day-care centre for elderly victims of Alzheimer's disease.' This information seemed to take the elders by surprise. 'In

Amewica,' continued Newo, 'appawently dwessed as a big woman.'

The grey-haired elder 'hmmmed' a bit. 'A Roman, you say … hmm.'

Newo shook his head. 'No, a woman.'

The ginger-haired lady leaned over. 'A woman, I think he said,' she whispered.

The grey-haired man looked even more surprised. 'A woman!' he exclaimed.

'Weawing a bwa,' added Newo. 'A wed Wonder Bwa.'

The elders all looked slightly embarrassed. 'Well then, we must rescue him,' said the grey-haired elder. 'Immediately, before he decides to stay like that.' The elders all nodded.

'It will be expensive getting to Iowa, both economically and emotionally,' said Newo. 'The weason that 99.999 per cent of the world does not live in Iowa, your honour, is because it is packed with … Amewicans. Huge fat Amewicans, hundweds of them. It is said, your honour, that Iowa actually weighs less than its population.'

The elders nodded. 'You are a brave man, Newo,' said the grey-haired elder.

'What about me?' demanded Titty.

'You are too, Titty darling,' he replied.

'We will fund your trip to Iowa. But you must make sure you bring back Amorphous or you will be confined to the stockade for the rest of your lives with only three decent meals a day,' explained the ginger woman.

'That's a little harsh,' said the grey-haired man. Newo agreed.

'Just try and get him back,' said the ginger woman, 'and don't bring him back dressed like a woman. I want the old Amorphous, the one some of us here have grown to … find interesting.'

Newo and Titty nodded, accepting the great task that lay before them.

'And don't get squashed by those fat Yanks,' said the grey-haired man as they turned and left.

CHAPTER EIGHT

GEEK SALAD

It was a long flight to Iowa. Newo and Titty could only afford to fly economy. The in-flight video told them they would arrive refreshed; the scriptwriters of the video had, however, omitted to add 'as a dog's arse', and they arrived absolutely shattered, with bad breath and aching from the small seats and zero leg room. They were met at the airport by Rank, who'd shipped the *Knobachaneza* over in a cargo ship via the Azores.

Des Moines airport was crawling with cops and Agent Provocateurs. Titty kept close to Newo.

'They're all watching us, Titty,' said Newo nervously.

Titty looked about at them. He was right: almost every person in the airport was staring at them suspiciously. 'I think maybe it's your dress, Newo,' she suggested. 'The erection probably isn't helping either.'

Newo tried to push it down a bit with his elbow while walking along. 'I'll get a modesty pouch in town later on.'

They exited the building and made their way to the car park. 'We could have got the bus like the others,' said Rank. 'It would save some time.' Titty and Newo watched as the bus pulled away from the terminal and stopped thirty feet down the road at the car park. Twenty or so massively overweight Humatonnes got out and wobbled over to their 4x4s. 'It appears that the average weight of a twelve-year-old girl in Des Moines is 26 stone,' explained Rank, 'with average sizes of 263–148–891. Not quite Kylie Minogue.'

They reached the *Knobachaneza* and got in. 'I have isolated twenty-seven care homes for elderly victims of Alzheimer's in the Des Moines area alone. America seems to have an awfully large number of people suffering from mental health problems,' explained Rank. 'Indeed, so serious is the problem that the line between the average American and those suffering from mental health problems such as total insanity has become blurred, to say the least, producing some terrifying effects. In many of the institutions I have identified it is almost impossible to tell the difference between the patients and the staff.' Rank swung the *Knobachaneza* out of the car park and headed off downtown.

'And what of Amowphous? Do you have any news of him?' asked Newo.

Rank shook his head. 'No sir, no sir, I don't.'

'I think perhaps we now face the gweatest challenge of all … finding Amowphous,' said Newo looking out of the window at all the enormous people.

'Well, let's not forget we have a rough idea of what we're looking for,' said Titty. 'A large, grossly obese woman, with enormous pendulous breasts, a smoker's cough and bad breath.'

Newo gazed at the locals milling around a car park as the *Knobachaneza* stopped outside a Wal-Mart. 'Look, Titty,' he said. 'Look out there at the locals.

Amowphous could be any one of them.'

Titty looked out of the window at the busy superstore car park jam-packed with massive obesity and respiratory health concerns.

'It will be like looking for a very small needle in a very large haystack,' said Rank as he pulled away from the lights shaking his head and looking depressed. 'It will be our greatest test.'

Five days and over 130 dead patients and staff later, Newo and Titty were beginning to think they might be onto something. They were waiting to be shown into the office of a man who went by the name of Mr Smiff. Newo and Titty had been led to understand that a vast mammoth of a woman who went by the name of Labertha Butternut-Squash had been employed just weeks before on the merits of her philosophy, but had almost immediately been removed from her position as director of the care centre and confined in a remote wing of the institution for an indefinite period after suggesting that humans had somehow been created by a process of evolution and natural selection and not by the Lord Jesus Christ. Indeed Labertha was only days away from having her head electrocuted off for her suggestions by the local governor, a one George U U Bush, a man whose blood lust knew no bounds.

'Mr Smiff will see you now,' said a small but incredibly shaped woman. Newo and Titty stood up and went into the office.

Smiff was sitting behind a desk grinning like he'd just got a blow job off Claudia Schiffer. 'Hello, Mr Sanderson. You weren't expecting me now, were you?'

Newo and Titty froze at the sight of him. 'What do you want, Smiff?' asked Newo, sitting down.

'I believe I should be asking the ... questions, Mr Sanderson ... I am after all the ... director here now ... hmm.' Titty stood behind Newo and clutched his chair nervously. 'I see you're still wearing your lovely flowery ... dress, Mr Sanderson ... hmm. And Ms Titty is looking as lovely as ever. Such a soft-looking rabbitskin merkin ... hmm.' Smiff sat back in his chair, grinning and staring at Titty's fanny.

'Where is he, Smiff?' demanded Titty coldly.

Smiff drew in a deep lungful of breath and sat forward, putting his palms together. 'I'm afraid that your … friend … Amorphous has been … incarcerated. It turns out that he is completely … insane. It tuns out that he holds various strange Darwinian notions concerning your … existence on this planet … hmm … when, as we all know … you are part of a scrolling green screensaver.'

'I suggest you tell us where he is, Mr Smiff,' said Newo, getting to his feet.

Smiff stood and squared up to Newo, smirking. Titty slowly slid her hand between her soft wet luscious callipygous, sorry, sorry, on her gun and cocked the trigger.

There was a knock on the door. 'Hmm … enter,' said Smiff. Another Smiff walked in, identical to the first in almost every way – indeed the only difference was that he had conjoined twin myslexia, a rare and horrific form of Siamese twin in which a sibling exists in embryo form attached to the host sibling. In Smiff's case the conjoined sibling was rather conveniently a martial arts expert called Ming. Newo and Titty jumped sideways as the double stepped into the room.

'Hello me,' said Smiff. 'Hello me,' replied the other Smiff.

Then from a cupboard emerged another Smiff, this one suffering from the same disfiguring form of myslexia, but his embryo resembled the popular American TV crimebuster Lone Wolf McQuade. 'Hello me,' said the first Smiff. 'Hello me,' said the third one. 'Hello me,' said the second to the third, and third replied, 'Hello me,' to the second.

'This is Lone Wolf,' said the third Smiff. 'He is helping me out with the whole Matewix thing in whatever way he can. He has expert tracking skills and, despite not actually having any legs or genitals himself, makes an excellent lover.' Lone Wolf looked a bit embarrassed. His position, protruding from Smiff's left buttock just level with his other 'man friend', was all just a bit embarrassing and suspicious. Titty looked over at him and he shrank back into Smiff's pubis and fiddled with his cowboy hat.

'Yes … anyway,' continued the first Smiff. 'You killed me, Mr Sanderson, you killed me by swallowing me whole. By rights, Mr Sanderson, I should not be here … hmmm … I should be *dead*. But … I came back, Mr Sanderson … I came back! I managed to … replicate myself … Admittedly I may have made a couple of minor … errors in the program … hence the little guys, Mr Sanderson, and the … legs being slightly bowed …' Newo and Titty looked at the legs of Smiffs Two and Three to see they had advanced rickets '… the two fingered hands …' Newo and Titty looked more disturbed '…and the total blindness.'

Newo and Titty looked closely at the replicas Smiff had made of himself, and noticed that they had no eyeballs. 'Yes,' said Newo. 'Well done.'

Another Smiff walked in. This one had a Russell Crowe embryo in full Maximus regalia sticking out of his thigh. 'My name is Maximus Decimus!' shouted the zygote, sticking a tiny little sword in the air. The Smiff who possessed him staggered forward through the door on his bow legs. 'Watch out!'

shouted Maximus Decimus, but it was too late and he banged his head on the corner of the cupboard.

'You see,' smiled Smiff, glowing with pride in his creations, 'the little guys can see perfectly.'

Newo looked at them pitifully. 'Lucky them,' he suggested.

Smiff dropped into his martial arts pose. 'So, to your question, Mr Sanderson, why am I here? ... You took something from me, Mr Sanderson, when you ate me ... and now I want it back ... hmm.'

Titty trained her gun on him. 'Make one move and I'll take your head off!' she hissed.

Smiff smiled and then pounced on Newo. He threw a fist straight into Newo's nose, knocking him backwards into Smiff Three. Titty fired twice into Smiff, but he swung round the bullets and smashed her backwards with a side kick.

'Left a bit, up a bit,' shouted Lone Wolf McQuade to Smiff Three. Smiff Three swung a fist or two into the air, but hit nothing. 'No, left, you dufus! That's your right!' growled the angry embryo.

Newo span round twice, kicking Smiff and Smiff

Two flying. Smiff Two landed in a cupboard on his side, squashing Ming, who let out a squeal.

'Forward about three feet,' ordered Maximus, thrashing about with his sword. Smiff Four staggered forward, while the tiny Roman attached to his left buttock thrust his sword forward, stabbing Newo in the knee. Newo span round and blocked Maximus' sword, but Maximus was fast and dodged all but Newo's best moves. Newo dropped to his knees to get level with the embryo.

'Take that and that and that!' shouted the wee man as he thrust his sword this way and that.

'Newo!' called Titty as Smiff Two staggered over to him, with Ming adopting his most powerful-looking kung fu stance.

'Left a bit more, now forward,' ordered the little guy. Titty turned her gun onto the crazy embryo and shot it twice, splattering it all over Smiff Two's pants. She then ran up the wall and kicked Smiff Two in the head. He fell sideways and she leaped onto him, battering him, while he flailed about totally unable to see.

'More of me and the embryo things!' shouted Smiff. The door burst open and more and more Smiffs staggered in, to a cacophony of squeaky voices saying, 'Forward, left a bit, right a bit.' Soon the room was full of them, all with their little guys. Newo and Titty were getting attacked from every angle. Newo's hands and feet were moving so fast that even if the Smiffs had been able to see him they wouldn't have been able to see his limbs moving. 'Now, now, now!' the embryos were all shouting to their masters as Newo's fists rained down, in the vain hope that they could perhaps block one of the punches from the Number Two, rather than just standing there being mercilessly battered.

Their shouts were useless. It wasn't long before the floor of the office was littered with the bodies of Smiffs and their embryos. Many of the embryos were still alive, and Titty was having to go round chopping their heads off with a big pair of scissors. Lone Wolf pulled out a tiny gun to try and fend Titty off, but it was only a toy one and so had no effect. Maximus Decimus was perhaps a little more effective in his defence, thrusting his sword at the scissors as they came at him, but Titty soon managed to snip his little arms off, so he was totally unarmed when she went for his head.

Newo interrupted Titty in her cold-blooded execution and dragged her off down the corridor. 'I can feel him,' he explained. 'Amowphous is close now. I can feel him.'

Titty dropped her scissors and composed herself. At the end of the green corridor they reached a door and turned left and right and left and right and left and right and left and right and left and right and left and right, until Titty said, 'Should we just go through the door rather than continuously walking into the wall on opposite sides of the corridor?'

Newo banged into the wall, turned right and banged into the other wall, turned left and did it again, before stopping to hold his head. 'Yes, it is getting wather painful,' he agreed, and pushed the door open. There was another long green corridor. They made their way down it until they got to another set of doors which opened onto another green corridor. 'Déjà vu,' said Newo.

'What did you say?' asked Titty.

'Déjà vu,' replied Newo.

'What did you see?' asked Titty, looking concerned.

'I saw one gween cowwidor … and then … I saw another gween cowwidor,' explained Newo.

'Was it the same gween cowwidor?' asked Titty.

Newo shrugged. 'I don't know,' he replied. 'They both look the same.'

Just then an old lady appeared at the end of the corridor. She wandered down towards Newo and Titty. 'Hello, Newo,' she said. 'Hello, Titty.' The two smiled at her and stood frozen as she stopped short of them. 'Would you like some jello?' she asked.

Newo thought for a moment. 'But you alweady know what I'm going to say, don't you?' he responded.

The old woman nodded and held out a fistful of blackcurrant jelly for Newo. Newo took her fist and ate the sweetened gelatine out of it. He seemed to like it and sucked and licked the old hag's fingers and palm until he'd got it all off. 'You're quite the man now, aren't you, Newo? I'm proud of you,' she said. Newo looked slightly embarrassed. 'You see, Newo, you are the Number Two. You know that now, though. I don't need to tell you. You have the sight now, Newo. But you already know that.'

Newo sort of shrugged and nodded at the strange woman. 'We're looking for a woman called Labertha Butternut-Squash,' he told her. 'Do you know her?'

The old woman smiled. 'But you already know I do,' she replied.

Newo shook his head. 'No, I don't. That's why I asked the question.'

The woman smiled. 'But I already knew what the question was.'

'Well, if you knew what the question was, why didn't you answer it?' asked Newo.

The woman smiled to herself. 'Because you already know the answer,' she replied. 'Not bright, though, is he?' she remarked to Titty. Titty nodded.

'But I don't know the answer. If I did I wouldn't have asked the question, would I?'

The woman smiled again. 'Where do you think you might find Ms Butternut-Squash, Newo?' asked the woman.

Newo shrugged and looked down the corridor. 'I don't know … down the cowwidor?' he ventured.

The woman smiled wryly. 'You see, Newo, you just need to see that you have the sight to see that you have the sight.'

Newo drew breath in frustration. 'Yes. Thanks for your help,' he said, smiling politely, before grabbing Titty's hand and dragging her off down the corridor, leaving the old woman nattering inanely to herself.

'She's quite the most insane person I've ever met,' whispered Newo to Titty as they burst through another set of green doors into another corridor. Titty tried to disagree but Newo talked over her. 'Acting like a bloody pwophet or something … Still, I suppose that's what Alzheimer's does – addles the bwain. Sad, weally.'

'Maybe she *was* a prophet,' argued Titty.

Newo laughed at Titty's naivety. 'Yeah, wight. If she's a pwophet I'm Keanu Weeves.'

They walked down the corridor looking through the windows of various doors to see mad old women saying 'You're no son of mine!' and cackling inanely to themselves. There were men as well. Newo could hardly hold his laughs in when he watched one old duffer trying to feed a Werther's Original to a standard lamp. 'Mad as a baboon,' he explained to Titty. At the end of the corridor was a room on the left. 'If that mad old hag was wight, Labertha Butternut-Squash should be in this woom,' he remarked to Titty. He sidled up to the window and peered through.

Inside was an enormous hulk of wobbling flesh. It appeared at first not to be human in any way, simply a large bulk of living flesh and fat deposits weighing a couple of tonnes. But it appeared to wobble a bit when it coughed, then a head popped up and looked through the window. 'Who is it?' asked the head. Newo and Titty continued to stare. The face was vast and round, lit by huge traffic light earrings and framed by a pearl necklace that could loop the earth at least twice. 'Who are you?' came a voice as dark and feminine as one could be without sounding like a grizzly bear.

Newo pushed the door open. 'My name is Newo,' he said. 'And you are?'

The blubber woman coughed and hacked until a bit of lung dislodged and popped into the back of her throat. She chewed on it a moment while viewing her guests suspiciously. 'The question is not "What is my name?" The question is "When is my name?"'

Newo caught Titty's eye. 'It's him!' he said. Titty nodded.

'What do you mean, "It's him!"?' demanded blubber woman. 'I'm a woman!'

'No you are not,' contradicted Newo. 'You are a man.'

The blubber woman wobbled her head. 'My name is Labertha Butternut-Squash and I am a woman.'

Newo looked back to Titty. 'Butternut-Squash!' he whispered. 'It is not! You're name is … Amowphous!'

Labertha's big ugly face turned angry. 'Well, I am not here to be believed … I am her because I believe,' she explained.

'Definitely Amorphous,' whispered Titty to Newo.

They moved further into the room, but there wasn't much floor space that Labertha hadn't utilized as storage for a thigh or an elbow. Newo tried to smile and not look at the flesh much, but he couldn't really help it. 'We have been looking for you, Labertha,' he explained. 'It seems you are a vewy special lady.'

Labertha dropped her jowls and eyed Newo with great suspicion. 'You aren't Norris McWhirter, are you?' she asked. 'From the *Guinness Book of Records*?'

Newo shook his head. 'We have nothing to do with wecords, Labertha.'

'Well, what are you here for then? To be brutally honest, if you're not here to feed me you can fuck off.'

Just then Newo noticed something scuttle across Labertha's stomach. It was sort of small and wiry with a slightly oversized head, Gollumesque if you will.

'What was that?' asked Titty, pulling her gun out.

'The question is not "What was that?" The

question is "When was that?"' replied Labertha.

Titty pointed the gun at her great face. 'The question was "What was that?"' she asked again, most forcefully.

'That was … Paul,' replied Labertha. 'He is my bitch. He … does things for me. You know, feeds me, wipes my, finds my …'

'Stop!' shouted Newo. 'Let's change the subject.' Newo watched as one of Labertha's vast thighs twitched a bit and a few ripples ran down her leg. Then a face appeared, a wormy little face with tall blond hair and blue eyes. It looked at Newo and then over to Titty. 'What is it, Titty?' asked Newo.

'It is my bitch,' replied Labertha.

'I don't know,' said Titty. 'It looks like Siphon in a funny sort of way. A worm-like, vegan, gardening version of Siphon.'

And then the bitch vanished, back into the labyrinth of cracks and folds.

'Sowwy. I digwessed,' continued Newo. 'We have been looking for you for a vewy long time, Ms Labertha. You are vewy special to us. It seems that you are ... not who you think you are. You are in fact someone entirely diffewent ... A MAN!'

Labertha looked thoroughly put out. 'Fuck off, you rude bastard. How dare you come in here calling me a man. I have a bealy. I saw it once. Granted it was a long time ago and I had to use a mirror on a stick, but it certainly was no man meat ... you rude bastard. Just because I'm massively overweight does not give you the right to come in here with you medical highbrow accusing me of being a goddam man. These look like man boobs to you?' She slapped her sides, making the entire coast of her chest wobble. Newo looked for nipples but couldn't see any, just large floppy nan breads which fell off the edge and went behind her back.

'Did you want to know what it is?' asked Newo, trying to remember what Amorphous had said to him.

'What what is?' demanded Labertha impatiently.

'The Matewix, Ms Butternut-Squash ... the Matewix.'

Labertha wobbled her head. 'No.'

Newo looked a bit stumped. 'I'll explain anyway. The Matewix is, almost, all awound you, although I'm not sure it is quite omni-accommodating. Still, much of you is suwwounded by it.'

'By what?' asked Labertha.

'A vast scweensaver,' explained Newo. 'A scweensaver so vast that you can't even see it.' Labertha looked sceptical, to say the least. 'You are a slave, Labertha, a slave in your own body.'

She looked furious. 'Fuck off with you again. How dare you? This is the U S of bloody A, mate. You don't say things like that. You tell me I'm a beautiful motherfucker, that's what you say. An' if I ain't on the outside I sure as hell is on the goddamn inside! This is a disease. I have a disease!' She blushed red with anger and wobbled like an angry elephant seal.

Newo looked slightly embarrassed. 'I didn't mean any offence,' he explained. 'Do you know the stowy of Alice, Labertha? Not the Amewican version, which was shortened considewably because Alice was unable to fit down the wabbit hole. The owiginal English version, witten by a known "fwiend of the

185

young", where Alice *did* go down the wabbit hole? Do you want to go down the wabbit hole, Labertha. Do you want me to show you just how deep it goes?'

Labertha shook her head. 'I want you to piss off. Out of my goddam room and out of my goddam life.'

Newo looked slightly disconcerted and looked to Titty for help. Titty smiled at the big woman. 'Would you like some tablets?' she asked. Labertha's face seemed to light up at the thought of medical treatment for her condition, rather than dieting and exercise.

Titty handed Newo a small pill box. He opened it and pulled out two pills, one red, one blue. 'I have two pills, Labertha, a blue pill and a wed pill. The blue pill will make you forget you ever met us and you will wake up later on forgetting any of this ever happened.'

'I'll have that one,' said Labertha, immediately understanding its benefits.

Newo was just about to explain the whole red pill rabbit burrow nonsense again but stopped and thought for a moment. 'Or you could take the wed pill. The wed pill will help you lose weight faster than you can possibly imagine. The tonnes will litewally dwop off you.' Labertha's face lit up. 'And you will be able to eat as much as you want for the west of you life and never get fatter than Clitowista Flockhard!'

'Paul!' shouted Labertha. 'Red pill, Paul.' The Gollumesque bitch appeared from her armpit and snatched the red pill out of Newo's hand before scuttling the few metres back across Labertha's chest and popping it into her mouth.

Newo put his hand out with some more red tablets. 'Give her a few,' he said. 'She's no Kate Moss, is she.'

'Rank!' shouted Newo down the phone. 'The trace is ready to go.'

Rank leaped out of the *Knobachaneza* and ripped the back open. He lowered a ramp and wheeled down the trace equipment, the ZX81s, the 4-litre Lister diesel engine. 'I'm on my way,' he called back down the phone and started pushing the trolley as hard as he could, into the institution and down all the green corridors.

Labertha was getting agitated by the time Rank pulled in. 'Why is I still a fat hoochie mumma then? You said I was going to be *all that*!'

'It takes a little while,' explained Titty.

Rank jumped onto Labertha and ran up her chest to attach a wire to her ear. She tried to thrash her arms about and fight him off, but it was pointless. 'Get off me, motherfucker!' she shouted. Rank turned to Newo.

'Just ignore her, Wank,' said Newo. 'She's too fat to do anything about it.'

Labertha looked furious and tried to thrash her head about, but it didn't really thrash, it sort of quivered. 'Paul!' she wailed. 'Get them off!'

The bitch leaped out of a fold under Labertha's inner thigh and started attacking Rank with scratches and bites. Rank tried to brush him off at first but the little guy was strong. He clambered onto Rank's back and started biting him in the back of the neck. Rank screamed in agony and danced about trying to get the bitch off him. Titty tried to aim her gun at Paul, but it was hard with all the movement. Rank managed to get hold of Paul's tall blond hair, though, and pulled him over his head with it, smashing him down on Labertha's enormous stomach with such force that he bounced up in the air and hit the ceiling. Titty shot him eight times in the head on the way down, splattering his brains all over Labertha's bosom. 'Aaagggghhhhh!' she screamed as she wobbled about trying to pull the leads out and get a bit of skull off her lip.

'She's going into cardiac arrest,' warned Titty.

Rank finished fixing her up with all the wires. He took a running jump off her stomach and landed on the floor next to the Lister.

'Huwwy up, Wank,' shouted Newo.

Rank pulled the start cord on the engine, but it did nothing. He rewound it and pulled again; the engine spluttered a bit, but died again. He rewound the cord another time and pulled again; nothing.

'We're losing her!' shouted Titty.

Labertha's vast body began to pulse and twitch.

Rank rewound the cable again.

'Let me do it, Wank,' said Newo, stepping up. He took the cord and calmly ripped it with all his might. The engine coughed a bit and fired into life.

'You see, Newo, you *are* the Number Two,' said Titty.

'No time for that,' relied Newo. 'Wank, the computer.'

Rank ran over to the ZX81 and pressed Play on the tape recorder that was attached to it. 'Shit, shit, shit,' he cursed.

'What is it?' asked Titty.

'The tape hasn't been rewound.'

Newo was furious. 'Wank, why hasn't anyone wewound the tape?'

'I don't know,' replied Rank as he hit Rewind. There was a brief silence while the tape rewound. Titty, Newo and Rank all smiled at each other and watched as Labertha's heart began spasming wildly.

'Do you think it *is* him?' asked Titty.

Newo shrugged. 'Yeah, it could be.'

'What if it's not?'

'Well, the world won't miss her.'

Labertha looked terrified. 'That old hag down the corridor said this would happen,' she spluttered. 'She said if I carried on eating like that I'd croak.' Labertha gasped for breath. 'Who does she think she is – a prophet or something? She's just a mad old hag … aaaagggghhhhh!'

'Huwwry up, Wank,' repeated Newo.

The tape reached the end and Rank hit Play. 'We've just got to wait for it to load now. It'll only take a couple of minutes.'

Newo clutched his temples in frustration. 'Come on! Come on!' he cursed.

The tape recorder started making all sorts of electronic noises. Newo and Titty watched the old TV screen monitor for signs of life. But life was rapidly vanishing from Labertha's vast body.

'We're in!' shouted Rank a few minutes later. He tapped with one finger on the keys. Labertha began making a horrific gurgling noise and farting very loudly and continuously as gas started to escape from her body.

'This is not good, Wank,' said Newo.

'It's OK, Newo ... nearly there, nearly there ... Got her!'

Labertha's body exploded into seizure. Her arms flew about with more strength than her conscious brain could ever muster and her legs kicked and thrashed, knocking Titty backwards onto her luscious, pert bottom.

Amorphous gasped as he sat up in his slop bucket. He pulled a sausage from his mouth and looked about. 'The question,' he said, 'is not "Why am I here?" I know why I am here. The question is "How long have I been here?"'

Just then one of those robots that disconnect the dead and the awake didn't appear, so Amorphous stayed where he was and worked out what to do. 'I must find the Cheese Maker,' he thought to himself. He began to unplug himself from the various tubes and wires that fed and held him, but just then one of those robot things didn't appear again so he carried on until he was unbondaged and stood up. Before him he could see miles and miles of equally stupid people in slop buckets. He swiped some of the beans and alphabet spaghetti off himself and climbed out of his bucket, leaning back in to grab a pork pie to munch.

And so Amorphous began his long climb from slop bucket to slop bucket in search of the Cheese Maker. He wandered and climbed for days, seeing many bizarre and interesting things, many of which he found rather exciting, and several people even nearly woke up as a result; but although he found many peculiar and intricate birth marks, he failed to find the Battle of El Alamein. He came very close on the fifth day when he found a woman with a map of Ypres straddling her breasts. And even closer on the seventh day when he was forced to vigorously thrust his sword into an almost perfect re-enactment of Battle of Bannockburn being played out on the bum of a young Scot.

It was a tiring and lonely business; hiding from the unplugging robot things and eating sausages out of people's slop. He forged on, though, driven by his own mindless delusions and mental health problems. 'My beliefs do not require me to believe that what I am doing is totally lunacy,' he kept saying to himself.

Eventually, after six weeks, his persistence paid off. He came across the arse of a man. He said sorry and brushed it off at first, but on closer inspection realized that the man was marked in a most violent way and that his member was very Monty-like – the vain, cocksure machismo and the battered helmet pointed in one direction. Indeed his nuts were not dissimilar to Rommel in many ways – the constant misfiring, the relentless battering and the hairy chin. He could see a couple of old Tommy tanks on the man's back and a few stiffs lying in a stain of defeat. 'I believe it must be,' he said to himself, 'and that, that must be, I believe *is*!'

Amorphous was nervous. He knew that if he woke the Cheese Maker from his stasis he would most certainly perish, as a body cannot live without its mind. But as he believed with the utmost conviction that whatever he did had to be done, by some sort of overpowering delusion, or 'fate' as he liked to call it, so it became his belief as he climbed into the slop bucket next to the Cheese Maker that, if he woke him up very gently, very slowly, his mind would perhaps be seduced out of the Matewix and his eyes would open in the real world. Amorphous thus had to conjure up some method of gently caressing and seducing the Cheese Maker away from the screensaver world and back into the world where Homo Erectus once roamed. The details of which I'm afraid I cannot share with you, as they are disturbing in the extreme and illegal in all but the poorest countries. I don't know if you've ever read *The Naked Lunch* by William Burroughs, but …

It was, however, the sight of Amorphous's 'real world' that threw the Cheese Maker's heart into almost instant cardiac arrest. Indeed the shock of waking up from a lifetime inside a computer-generated world was negligible in comparison to what he saw Amorphous doing behind his back. And thus the Cheese Maker's foray into the real world was cut painfully short. Amorphous wept on his bosom when he realized what he'd done, but continued to believe that, because *he'd* done it, it was the right thing to do and the thing that must have been done. It wasn't until he consoled himself with the certain pleasures he'd endured that he raised himself up and realized something. The man was not actually the Cheese Maker! Upon a closer examination Amorphous realized that Rommel actually appeared to have the upper hand and Monty was limp beneath him. 'This can't be El Alamein,' he said to himself. 'Rommel's winning!'

The episode had weakened Amorphous's resolve, however, and he finally conceded that he should return to Llanfairpwllgwyngyllgogerychwyrndrobwllllantysiliogogogocock for a bit of R & R before continuing his quest for the Cheese Maker.

Newo and Titty were already there when Amorphous staggered into Llanfairpwllgwyngyllgogerychwyrndrobwllllantysiliogogogocock. They hadn't really given Amorphous a thought for days, to be honest, but they pretended to be very happy to see him when he rolled in.

'Amowphous!' exclaimed Newo. 'Where have you been? We gave you up for dead.'

Amorphous seemed slightly humbled. Perhaps he had disturbed himself by crossing boundaries he had previously been unaware of the existence of. 'I have returned. I have returned … empty-handed.' He held out his bare palms.

'Where have you been?' asked Titty.

'I have plumbed the power plant from darkest depth to highest peak, searched every breathing body, plundered every corpse. But I have not found the Cheese Maker.'

Newo and Titty looked slightly disturbed. 'Well, you're back now. Would you like a cup of tea?' asked Titty.

Amorphous nodded. 'The question is not "Will", it is "When". "When will I have a cup of tea?"'

Titty flicked the switch on the kettle. 'Not long, a couple of minutes.' She set about getting a cup.

'We thought we had lost you, Amowphous. All our signals suggested you had … died. Wank even made a special coffin to bewwy you in. Yes, a special coffin.

But it was so large that we couldn't get it out of the woom. So Titty blew up the institution and we bewwied you like that.'

Amorphous looked surprised. 'Did you speak with the Mystic Mog, Newo?' he asked.

Newo looked down at his feet. 'Ah yes, the Mystic Mog. Yes. To be honest, I think we all got a wee bit cawwied away with the whole Mog thing. I think in hindsight that, well, that she was just some old woman's cat, not weally the omniscient, pwophesying being we cwedited her with being.'

Amorphous looked irritated. 'The truth, Newo, is not an object that can be moulded. Not an object that you can fashion or manipulate to your own opinion and belief. The Mog is the Prophet, Newo. And whether you believe that or not, *it is*.' Newo looked slightly doubtful in the hope that Amorphous would somehow see though his lunacy. 'So where is the Mog?' asked Amorphous.

'The Mog is cuwwently, well, what she did was, she died.'

Amorphous staggered back, horrified. 'Dead?' he

shrieked. 'Dead? It cannot be true. That is not in the prophecy.'

Newo clicked his cheek. 'Yeah, it's a bugger, isn't it? Still, these things happen. They say a cat has nine lives – that's a pwophecy, but, like our pwophecy, it turned out to be, well, wong. The cat had one life.'

Titty gently placed a cup of tea on the table for Amorphous. 'How did she die?' he enquired. 'What power so strong could annihilate such a being?'

'Titty's gun, as it happens. It was of course a dweadful mistake, but the Mog should have seen it coming, to be honest, and it is with this evidence that I pwesent to you the theowy that she may thus have been just a cat.' Amorphous looked shocked. 'Indeed, it is only with hindsight that I have come to believe that the old hag from the institution may have been the Pwophet. I thought she was as mad as a dog when I met her, widdled with Alzheimer's. She dwibbled absolute twoddle. But it appears that she suggested events that have since happened, with an astonishing accuwacy. So it is perhaps the mad old hag that we should be following wather than the ginger cat.'

Amorphous looked interested and surprised. 'The Mog told me this would happen,' he said in a tone of triumph. Titty and Newo nodded sympathetically. 'Well then, we must meet this mad prophet. We must meet her at once. Because I have failed to find the Cheese Maker, and I therefore seek guidance … Where is she?'

'Ah,' replied Newo. 'Dead also.'

'Dead?' wailed Amorphous. 'Dead?'

'Yes. Died at your funewal. Titty, you see … she sort of detonated a vewy large bomb and sort of bewwied evewyone in the institution; being old they would have died soon anyway, but, yes, the Pwophet pewished along with them when sevewal hundwed tons of hardcore landed on her bwittle little body.'

Amorphous shook his head and took a masterly stroll. 'I'm gone five minutes,' he cursed to himself, 'five minutes.'

Newo and Titty stood stock still, feeling like idiots. 'But there again, if she had been a pwophet she would have seen it coming and perhaps stood aside when the wubble came down … So, you see, in hindsight my hindsight was wrong!' explained Newo.

Amorphous stopped his stroll and glared at him. 'No, Newo, what has happened is that you and Titty have killed two prophets.' Newo and Titty tried to smile. 'And did they suggest anything to you before you murdered them? Where it's going to end? Where the Cheese Maker is?'

Newo and Titty shook their heads. 'No, wait,' said Newo. 'The Mog, she had a number on hew tag. It was 'Burglar King nine, four, nine, seven, fwee, two.'

Amorphous nodded, not surprised by what he heard. 'You see, your eyes, Newo, they tell your mind what they think it needs to know. But the truth, Newo, the truth is in there already. You didn't believe that the Mog was a prophet, but the Mog was. 949 732 is a grid reference, Newo.'

'A gwid wefewence?'

'Yes, a *Grid Reference*, Newo. It is the code, Newo. The code to the Merrill Lynch. The code to the Cheese Maker!'

CHAPTER NINE

GEEK IS THE WAY WE ARE FEELIN'

Council was held in Llanfairpwllgwyngyllgogerych-wyrndrobwllllantysiliogogogocock on the night of Amorphous's return. It seemed that something pressing had begun to press considerably harder. The grey-haired gentleman and the ginger lady were of course leading the discussion, as all the other elders spoke a form of Welsh so broad that no one else could make any sense of it – not even themselves! And all the captains and pilots of every milk float and ice cream van were there, including Nairobi and her crew.

'Welcome home, Amorphous,' said the ginger elder. 'It's good to have you back.'

Amorphous nodded courteously. 'Thank you,

ma'am. It is my belief that it is good to be back.'

There was a semi-unanimous cheer, if there can be such a thing, and many of the more Welsh pilots and captains broke briefly into close harmony, singing, 'Welcome home, welcome home, welcome home, welcome home, Amorphous, you big poof, you big poof, you big poof.' Attention which was not lost on Amorphous, who lapped it up as if it were 'attention milk', if there can be such a thing.

'There is a matter far graver than close harmony pressing on us this night,' said the grey-haired elder as the badly constructed and badly sung song ground to an end. 'As we speak there is an army descending upon us.' Newo looked at Titty, slightly confused. 'The Bentanals are bearing down upon us. As we speak thirty or so are closing in,' explained the grey-haired elder.

'But that's one for every person in here!' shouted the young captain, getting a bit worried and excited.

'It is, young captain. This is the corner of our concern.' The grey-haired elder held his hands aloft. 'Does anyone here have any bright ideas?'

Amorphous held forth. 'The Bentanals will never make it, your honour.'

The council eyed Amorphous carefully. He seemed to know something. 'How do you know that?' asked the ginger elder.

'My beliefs do not require me to know it, your honour,' he replied.

'Yes. Sit down, Amorphous,' said the grey-haired elder dismissively.

'But we have the Number Two!' protested Amorphous, pointing to Newo. Newo looked embarrassed and sort of smiled and tried to shrink.

'Stand up, Newo, let's take a look at you,' said the grey-haired elder. Newo unfolded himself from his chair and stood up. 'It is said, Newo, that you are the Number Two. What do you suggest we do?'

Newo thought for a moment. He looked back to Titty for support. She smiled at him seductively and pushed her breasts together to form a luscious cleavage. Newo's dress rose up a bit more and he turned to address the council. 'I think Amowphous is wight!' he said.

'He's clearly black,' argued the ginger lady. 'Look at him.'

'I think he means *right*,' offered the grey-haired elder. 'It's just his absurd speech impediment. Continue, Newo.'

Newo straightened his dress a little over his horn. 'It seems that ever since I have been coming to Cock, the Bentanals have been pwessing down on us, just seconds away fwom total annihilation. They never seem to appear, though. I often wonder whether they ever will, your honour. Or whether we are all just mistaken. A lot has happened since my first visit to Cock. Amowphous has exposed me to a whole world I never dared to expewience. I have spent weeks ducking in and out of the Matewix, I have spent days learning skipping and mud-westling techniques, I have even gone on a fwee-day watercolour painting course. All this, and yet fwom the vewy first day I awwived, and evewy day since, I have been told that the Bentanals are just hours away.' The elders looked agitated. 'So I …'

'Yes. Sit down now,' interrupted the grey-haired

elder. 'If you don't have anything sensible to say, don't say anything. Anyone else got anything to say?'

Newo sat down in embarrassment. Amorphous stood up boldly. 'I must find the Cheese Maker!' he said forcefully. 'I must find the Cheese Maker and destroy the Matewix!'

The elders all looked at each other and whispered. 'But the man is a complete arsehead,' replied the grey-haired man.

'That he might be, your honour.'

'He once tried to play a Dairy Lea triangle in the school musical,' chipped in Valerie Maplesyrup.

Amorphous nodded. 'Yes, he might have done that as well. He is no doubt a very unpleasant individual … but he is as an integral part of our mission. Without the Cheese Maker we cannot destroy the Matewix.'

'May I ask why?' asked the ginger-haired elder.

'I believe that is for the Cheese Maker to know and for us to believe,' replied Amorphous.

'Are you saying that you don't actually know, Amorphous?'

Amorphous looked a little embarrassed. 'My beliefs do not require me to believe that I don't know.'

'Well, mine do,' replied the ginger-haired woman. 'So, once again: Do you know why the Cheese Maker is so crucial in the destruction of the Matewix?'

Amorphous looked about nervously. 'The Matewix is all around us. It is the air we breathe, it is the chairs we sit on. You are a slave, a slave in your own mind. The Mate—'

'Mr Amorphous!' boomed the grey-haired elder. 'Just answer the question. Of what importance is this Cheese Maker?'

'He is … Plato once noted that … actually I don't know.' Amorphous looked down at his feet, embaresed.

'Well then, how do you know he is so integral?' asked the ginger elder.

'The Mog told me,' explained Amorphous.

'What? An elderly ginger domestic cat, belonging to an old woman who lived in the suburbs of Slough?' demanded the ginger-haired elder.

'Yes,' replied Amorphous.

'Well, why didn't you say? We must move immediately. Captain, I want all your vehicles ready to accompany Amorphous and the *Knobachaneza* to find the Cheese Maker as soon as possible.'

The young captain stood up in a fury. 'This is madness!' he protested. 'We are about to be attacked by a vast army of killer robots and you want to send our entire defence off in search of a man who makes cheese; who, according to some old bird's moggy, is the only bloke capable of destroying some imaginary screensaver. Madness! Sheer madness!' The young captain was shaking with rage.

'*Captain!*' bellowed the grey-haired elder. 'Stand down, captain. You are out of order.' The captain shrank back a bit. 'We'll keep one vehicle back, then. Is there anyone who will volunteer to stay?'

Everyone put their hands up. 'What, everyone?'

Everyone nodded and said 'Yes.'

The elders looked slightly infuriated. 'Well, is there anyone who will go with the *Knobachaneza*?' There was silence and everyone looked about at everyone else.

'Not one?' asked the ginger bird. There was an uncomfortable silence as everyone convinced themselves that going was suicide.

'Come on, you bunch of fannies!' said the grey-haired elder. 'It's not far to Clitheroe from here. You'd get there within two days. It's only up the M6.'

The captains and pilots all began to chat among themselves.

'There's a Little Chef on the way,' suggested the ginger woman.

Nairobi's hand immediately shot into the air. 'Ah'll go, motherfuckers. Naawhaamsayin.' The chatter stopped as everyone turned to Nairobi. 'I ain't no fat hoochie momma. I am one hundred per cent Third World punanie, I all dat! Motherfuckers.'

Much of this was lost on the more Welsh elders. 'Nairobi will go … good,' said the grey-haired elder.

Phil Offeastenders buried his head in his hands at the thought of spending more time in the Mr Whippy, listening to Steak Fork's relentless banter with young girls and Nairobi's incessant questioning of the Matewix, a concept she was totally unable to grasp because she was a woman.

'You must leave in the morning. I wish you luck,' said the grey-haired elder.

'We will leave immediately,' said Amorphous.

'No!' protested Steak Fork. 'I need to stock up on flakes and Big Feet.'

LOCATION: Burglar King, Clitheroe High Street
Amorphous, Titty and Newo were getting odd looks as they made their way up the High Street. Laura Ashley dresses on men with erections are generally frowned upon in the less liberal North; as are gorgeous brunettes wearing a single blue tit feather over their private parts. They had a few remarks thrown at them, none very nice, and were even accosted by two very angry old women who told them they were 'disgusting' until Titty was forced to shoot them both in the head; at which point they both went very quiet.

They turned into Burglar King and threw the double glass doors open. Since this was the North, the Burglar King was packed. Everyone turned to watch as the bizarre trio entered and strolled about as if they owned the place.

Amorphous went up to the counter, ignoring the queue. 'I am looking for the Merrill Lynch,' he said to the spotty teenager behind the counter.

'Would you like fries with that?' replied the boy.

'I am looking for the Merrill Lynch,' repeated Amorphous.

'Regular or large?'

Amorphous sighed deeply. 'I am looking for the Merrill Lynch. Do you know where he is?' he said, very irritated.

'Do you want to go large?' asked the youth, apparently totally unable to use his tiny brain for anything other than serving flattened cow and horse ventricle to the masses.

Amorphous grabbed the spotty shit by the throat and dragged him half over the counter. 'You are a slave,' he said. 'You are a slave, you burger-serving fuck!'

Titty immediately shot the youth in the head and he fell to the floor.

'Get the regional manager!' shouted Amorphous to the other staff, brushing aside a young girl who ran over, screaming and hugging the corpse of her burger-flipping love.

Newo went up to a till while the staff went off to find the duty manager. 'Could I get a Chicken Woyale with wegular fwies and onion wings?'

The girl at the checkout looked at him in confusion. 'We only do chicken wings, we don't do onion wings,' she said.

'No, onion *wings*,' explained Newo.

'Sorry, sir, we don't do onion wings, only chicken wings.'

Titty ripped her gun from beneath her blue tit feather and fired three times into the girl's chest. She then leaped over the counter and grabbed a brown paper bag, into which she shoved a Chicken Royale, some regular fries and some onion rings. She shoved it onto the counter next to Newo, who accepted it and took it over to a nearby table.

The regional manager came out with a short lizard-like woman who was sucking on a Lambert

Menthol. The man was portly and red faced, with wispy grey hair and mutton chops like John Bull. 'Aye,' he said in a broad Yorkshire accent. 'What can'a doo for yoo then, lad?' he asked.

'We are looking for the Merrill Lynch,' replied Amorphous.

'Aye, that's me, lad,' replied the Yorkshireman.

Amorphous viewed him suspiciously. 'The Merrill Lynch is rumoured to be half American, half Argentinian and two-thirds Dutch,' he said.

'Aye,' replied the Yorkshireman.

'You appear to be over 1000 per cent Northern … sir,' replied Amorphous.

'Aye,' replied the Merrill Lynch. 'An this is ma waf Shirley.'

Amorphous became a little confused. 'We are searching …'

'I know wha yer here, lad. A'might be from Yorkshire bot it doesn't mean I'm stoopid in the ed, does it, lad?' replied the Merrill.

'Where is he then?' asked Amorphous.

'Ya can't have him. Ee's mine. Now fock off!'

Newo finished his burger, chips and onion rings and stood up. 'I suggest you tell us where he is, Mr Lynch,' he said, trying to look big in front of Amorphous.

Some of the staff and customers shrank further back out of view. Titty put her hand on her gun. The Merrill Lynch walked out from behind the bar in a masterly way. '¿Que pasa aqui ahora? Ah blody lov Spanish, me. It's blody gret. Translated it means, "Do ya know wha' yer here, lad?"' he asked, looking at Newo.

'We are here to find the Cheese Maker,' interrupted Amorphous.

'Wrong-g!' shouted the Yorkshireman. 'Yoo are here, lad, because you were told to come here. You were told to come here by a cat. So yah did, lad. That's wha' yer ere, intit?' Amorphous shook his head in disagreement. 'Aye, lad, it's true. Bot tha Cheese Meker, lad, the Cheese Meker is not a reason, the Cheese Meker is a means, lad, a means. The question therefore, lad, is, What is the Cheese Meker a means to? ¿Que es los conclucioanos de creator a queso?' With this the fat Northerner slumped down in one of the Burglar King regulation chairs.

'You know the answer to that question,' said Newo.

'$E = MC^2$, lad. That's why yer ere, lad!'

'We are here to find the Cheese Maker,' repeated Amorphous.

'Relativity, lad. Each action as an equal an opposite reaction,' explained the Merrill.

'That's not welativity,' replied Newo. 'Welativity is the theowy that energy is equal to mass, multiplied by the square of the velocity of light.'

The Yorkshireman looked slightly put out. 'Look ere, lad. Yer not listening, are ya? Each action as an equal an opposite reaction.' The Merrill's eyes scouted about the restaurant. 'Tek that bloke, that fat bastard over there. Look at im, so normal, so blody borin and fat. So English. Ee's stoffin is fece whi burgers, lad … burgers and fries.' Everyone turned to look at the bloated man as he threw his chops around half the bap. 'Bloody greedy bastard! Anyway, equal an opposite. That burger ees eatin. I med that whi the

special secret Burglar King recipe. Watch im whi it as
ee stoffs is fece.' Everyone watched again. 'Ee'll start
feelin shite soon. Ee'll feel sick, like ee's eaten
somethin fattnin and greasy med a really low-grade
meat.' The man appeared to start feeling queasy, and
wiped his blubbery mouth. 'Then the guilt will set in,
lad, great fockin swathes o' it.' The man slumped
back in his chair, clutching his stomach. 'Then
somethin'll appen, lad. That fat bastard's body'll
reject it, lad. Cos it's shite.' The man started going
red and convulsing a little. 'Each action, lad ... each
action as an equal an opposite reaction.' The fat
bloke suddenly lurched forward and vomited all over
his mother. She screamed and jumped up, flicking and
wiping off the bits of soggy lettuce, tomato and
gherkin. 'Equal an opposite, lad! Equalisimo de
opposita! So you see, lad, you were told to com ere
by a cat, an yah did ... Now I'm tellin ya ta fock off,
and ya will! Equal an opposite.'

Amorphous stood firm. 'We seek the Cheese
Maker,' he said again.

'Well ya can't ave him. Ee's mine. There's no one

else in the whole of tha North oo can mek cheese like that lad. Mek it so square, so flat, that it sits on the burgers so perfectly. If I lost tha Cheese Meker, I wouldn't be able to mek arf ponders whi cheese, now would I? So yah not avin im.' The Merrill Lynch got up and walked off.

'Where are you going?' asked Amorphous.

'For a shite. Now fock off!' he shouted over his shoulder and vanished behind a staff-only door.

Shirley hung about on the end of her Lambert Menthol looking slightly embarrassed.

'We are looking for the Cheese Maker,' said Amorphous to her.

'Oh, im!' she said. 'Ee's out back makin cheese slices.'

'Will you show us where we can find the Cheese Maker?' asked Amorphous.

'Yeah, all right,' said the lizard.

Amorphous, Titty and Newo followed as she went off behind the counter and through a set of double doors. She led them through the kitchen and into the ladies' loos out back. When they were all in she stopped and turned to them. 'You gotta do somethin for me, though, intit,' she said, looking at Titty.

'What?' asked Amorphous.

'I've seen the way you look at im,' she said to Amorphous of Newo. 'I've seen the look in your eyes. They glint, the passion that you'd lov ta snog im whi.' Amorphous looked a little embarrassed and Newo stepped back a little. 'Well I want the bird to snog me like you want to snog im.'

'You want me to snog you with the passion he wants to snog him with?' asked Titty.

'Aye,' replied the lizard. She smiled broadly, showing off her set of broken yellow dog-end teeth and sucking hard on her menthol. Titty looked at Amorphous and then at Newo. 'Are ya gem then, bird?' asked the lizard. 'I'm like a lezzer, see.'

Titty ripped her pistol out and aimed it straight at Shirley's head. 'Open your mouth one more time and I'll shoot a hole in it!' she said nervously.

Amorphous put a hand over her arm and lowered the gun. 'You must do it, Titty,' he said. 'You must frenchy the old hag.'

Titty relaxed her pistol arm and tried to look away as the lizard smiled again and stood there waiting.

'Ya know yah want to, lov,' said the lizard.

Titty stepped forward slightly. 'You must tongue her, Titty, if we are to find the Cheese Maker and destroy the Matewix.'

Titty realized her responsibility and craned her neck towards Shirley. Shirley grinned like a shit-eater and grabbed the back of Titty's head, slamming her face into it and shoving her tongue down her throat. Titty squirmed and gasped as the hag sucked her tongue out of her mouth into her own and clasped it between her teeth, sucking the life out of it.

Three minutes later the hag released her and Titty collapsed in a heap to the floor. The hag stood there panting and smiled at Amorphous. Amorphous smiled and looked at Newo lovingly. Newo smiled very nervously and stepped back. Titty gasped for breath and wobbled a bit as she tried to find her feet.

'Stand, Titty,' commanded Amorphous. Titty forced herself to her feet and wiped her mouth and tongue repeatedly with her arm. 'Now you must show us where the Cheese Maker is,' said Amorphous.

Shirley nodded and walked off towards the back of the toilets. She pressed the button on the air hand dryer and a secret door appeared. They stepped through it and found themselves in a small back yard full of rubbish and building material. The hag stepped over the clutter and made her way to a small outside privy at the other end of the yard. On the door of the privy was a small sign that said 'The Dairy'. There was a very strange odour coming from the shed, a sort of Parmesan versus Scampi Flavoured Fries smell. Shirley unlocked the padlocked door and pushed it open.

Inside the tiny toilet shed was a man with a tongue-scraper wire collecting cheese. I shan't tell you how. But he leaped to his feet and pulled his pants up as the door opened. 'Hello. I'm the Cheese Maker,' he said. 'I've been expecting you.' He held out his hand excitedly for Newo to shake. Newo politely declined as he could see the man was clutching a half-full jam jar of something or other in the other hand.

'I must see your arse,' said Amorphous. 'I must be sure you are the Cheese Maker.' The Cheese Maker looked a little embarrassed. 'I must see your arse,' repeated Amorphous. The Cheese Maker put his jar down and turned around, pulling his pants down to show off his arse. 'There it is!' whispered Amorphous as the full, perfect replication of the Battle of El Alamein appeared before him. 'And your cock,' said Amorphous. The poor man turned to show everyone his organ. 'There he is!' whispered Amorphous as an almost perfect vision of an upside-down Montgomery swung into view.

The Cheese Maker pulled himself up. 'Now can we go?' he asked.

Amorphous, Titty and Newo jumped into life. 'Yes, we must,' said Amorphous.

They made their way back towards the Burglar King, following Shirley across the cluttered yard and through the women's bogs. The Merrill Lynch was waiting for them, though, out in the restaurant. He was standing there, all fat and Yorkshire and proud, with a couple of scabby teenagers for protection.

'Ow can ya doo this to me, lov?' asked the Merrill of his Shirley. 'Betray me so. ¿Mi amour mon chouffler de belleismo fetechini de la sun dried tomato?'

Shirley looked a bit embarrassed and sucked two-thirds of a Butler in one enormous hard suck. 'Equal an opposite, lov,' she replied as a cumulus of smoke billowed from her lungs.

'What equal, what opposite, lov?' he begged of her.

'A'm a lezzer, Merrill,' she explained. The Merrill looked horrified. 'That's what's equal, lov. Equal blody raghts. I know ma blody rights, lov … an I wanted to snog that bird. So I did, lov. I practically tongued er longs, lov. Ooo, it were so passionate, lov.'

The Merrill shook his head, still unable to work out what was equal and opposite to his wife's new-found lesbianism. 'Ya disappoint me, lov. Nah get opstairs and watch *Women in Lov* on the box, get som kinky stoff on and I'll be op for a shandy in a cople of minutes.'

Shirley put out her fag and vanished off up the stairs.

'You two, get the Cheese Maker,' said the Merrill to the two spotty youths.

'I'm not going back into that shed,' said the Cheese Maker and sank back into the wall.

'Don't worry,' said Titty. 'We'll look after you.'

Amorphous turned towards the door to the women's toilets, grabbed the Cheese Maker by the arm and shot out through it. Titty followed. Newo stepped forward, smiling. The spotty youths brushed past him and charged through the door into the women's bogs. A couple more spotty youths joined the Merrill at his side and sort of looked about, unable to make eye contact. 'Get him!' shouted the Merrill.

The two lads ran at Newo. Newo leaped onto the counter with a somersault and landed with legs straddling a till. The lads grabbed at his feet but Newo was too fast; he bounded into the air, knocking the two boys' skulls together with his feet. They fell to the floor moaning, clutching their temples. Newo skipped along the counter, lifting the corner of his dress with his thumbs and index fingers.

The Merrill regarded him with contempt. 'OK, ya seem to ave a couple of moves.' He was joined by three more spotty teenagers, all wearing the regulation red T-shirts with 'I live to serve' written across a smiley face motif, with a red cap sporting the same logo and a pair of blue slacks covered in grease and flour stains. 'Bot lads, don't forget ee's still yooman, ee's no a blody Yorkshireman!'

The lads ran towards the counter. Newo laughed as they neared him and skipped onto the ceiling, where he scuttled about like a cockroach, kicking the strip lights onto the Merrill Lynch and pulling off all the hanging adverts for the various mechanically recovered meat-based products on offer, including the Sound of Music Flamer, which included not only some dilute sugar syrup and chips, but also a mat of processed chicken shit in a bap with Von Trapp lettuce and Julie Andrews mayonnaise.

The teenagers and the fat Yorkshireman all ducked as the ceiling rained down on them. 'Get that quir bastard, lads!' he shouted as Newo kicked the air-conditioning unit off at the Merrill. It was getting difficult up there, though; Newo's dress, under the force of gravity, had fallen inside out over his head and he was practically blinded by it, relying almost solely on the powers of the Number Two to navigate and causing mass hysteria below as he didn't appear to be wearing any pants.

It was almost all over when one of the spotty youths climbed onto the counter and grabbed Newo by the dress. It was his last move. Newo cartwheeled off the ceiling, kicking the lad in the head and snapping his neck. He landed on the floor by the counter and squared up as the other two youths came on. One attacked him with a mop handle and the other with a bap slice, but Newo grabbed the mop and turned it on them both, pummelling them in the face with the soggy end.

Amorphous, Titty and the Cheese Maker had their hands equally full. After a brief scuffle in the girls' loos, Amorphous had held the youths off with a toilet brush; but it soon dripped so much onto Amorphous's leg that he had to abandon it and the three had been forced to run again. The youths were fast, and it was only the sight of Titty's incredible buttocks that kept them from catching up.

Fortunately Amorphous's Astra was near by. The Cheese Maker and Amorphous jumped in, while Titty held the lads off by bending over at the driver's side door. The boys stood frozen for a moment, giving Amorphous and the Cheese Maker the chance to buckle up. Then Titty jumped in to take the wheel. She fired the 1.2 litre engine into life and sped off up Clitheroe High Street at over 28 miles an hour. The lads ran out into the High Street after the car and jumped on the number 43, which was conveniently waiting at the bus stop. It wasn't a fair race by any stretch of the imagination. The Astra was restricted by a traffic calming scheme limiting it to 25 mph, while the bus was free to travel at 30 mph – in a bus lane!

'Get us out of here, Rank,' shouted Amorphous down the phone. Rank scanned his screens for an escape route.

'I've got you a line on … actually it's on the Isle of Skye!' he called back to Amorphous.

'Have you got anything closer? Skye is over 300 miles from here, Rank.'

Rank had another look. 'I've got a line in Solihull. That's only a few miles away.' Amorphous thought about it for a moment as Titty skidded round a corner. 'The views on the way to Skye would be significantly better,' offered Rank down the phone.

'The M6 North!' shouted Amorphous to Titty as she came to a motorway roundabout sign. 'I'm not going to Solihull!' declared Amorphous. 'I'd rather die!'

Titty squealed round the roundabout and shot off down the slip road.

'But, sir, the motorway … you said never the motorway … especially the M6 at rush hour on the last day of the school holidays!' shouted Rank.

'It's true,' remarked Titty. 'You said never the motorway, you said it was suicide!'

Amorphous nodded. 'Let's hope I was wrong.'

The Astra joined the slow lane and tried to pick up speed, but it didn't really have any so it crawled for a while.

'The youths!' warned the Cheese Maker.

Amorphous turned to see the 43 bearing down on them, just 400 yards away. 'Step on it, Titty, you filthy bitch. Step on it!'

Meanwhile Newo was repeatedly battering the last of the youths with a life-size cutout of the band Blazin Squad who appeared to be advertising Pepsi as they were unable to sing. The poor lad was squirming and writhing beneath the stiff cardboard as it smashed against him, banging his head against the till and the straw dispenser. 'Take that and that and that!' shouted Newo. The boy eventually slumped to the floor as his neck broke. Newo turned and looked across the carnage at the Merrill Lynch.

'This is not over, lad. Aye, it's not blody over. I survived Keith Chegwin, lad. Ee were yer predecessor, lad. Ee were a Number two an all – wanker!' The Merrill Lynch stormed off through the main doors. Newo ran after him and burst through the doors – only to find himself in a completely different place.

'Where am I, Wank?' he shouted down his phone. Rank scanned the screens.

'Runcorn!' he replied. 'You appear to be on Runcorn High Street!'

Newo swung round, looking at the high street. 'Wuncorn!' he shouted. People were beginning to stop and stare; they didn't often see men with dresses and erections. 'Get me out of here, Wank. Where are the others?'

'You need to go 100 miles due north. They're on their way to the Isle of Skye.'

Newo spotted a taxi rank and ran over to it. 'Get me to the neawest airport,' he said as he jumped in.

'Agent Provocateurs!' shouted Titty. She swerved the car across the motorway into the middle lane. The Agent Provocateurs turned after her, ramming a Volvo out the way. It appeared to be Cline and Beacham, piloting a Hyundai Lantra.

'Heads down!' called Amorphous as Cline took aim with his gun and fired at the car. The bullets seemed to miss completely and Titty screeched across to the fast lane. 'Put your foot on it, Titty!' shouted Amorphous.

'I am, I am,' she replied. 'This car only does 65, and the speed limit's 70 anyway.'

Beacham rammed a white van out of his path and drew up behind the Astra in the fast lane. 'Head down again,' warned Amorphous, and another hail of bullets sailed safely by.

'They've got their sunglasses on,' said Titty. 'They obviously can't see very well.' Amorphous went for the glove box. 'What are you doing?' asked Titty.

'Getting mine on,' replied Amorphous. 'I haven't worn them since Iowa.' He pulled them out and put them on.

'Nooooo!!!!' wailed Titty. 'Now's not the time, Amorphous.'

Suddenly the car rocketed forward, jolting the passengers, as the Hyundai smashed into the back of it.

'Where are they?' asked Amorphous, looking about but unable to see very much.

Titty shook her head. 'Behind us.'

Amorphous ripped out his gun and started randomly firing in all directions, sending bullets everywhere, often into the heads of innocent road users, at the Agent Provocateurs and around the inside of the car.

'Amorphous!' shouted Titty. 'You'll kill us all!'

Out of nowhere the 43 bus was upon them. It drew up on the passenger side in the middle lane and began swerving across the carriageway at the Astra. Titty tried to accelerate, but the car had little left to give. It appeared that the spotty youths had taken control of the bus and were bent on murder.

'Take the wheel,' called Titty to Amorphous as the Agent Provocateurs came in from behind, all guns blazing. Amorphous lent over and fumbled around for the wheel while Titty climbed into the back.

'What are you doing?' he shouted.

'I'm going to slow the boys down.' She got onto the seat, ripped off her blue tit feather and pressed her beautiful arse up against the window. The Agent Provocateurs suddenly stopped firing as they sat back, shocked, beholding an object of such beauty. The bus then dropped back and hung behind the Astra, alongside the Agent Provocateurs, as the two spotty youths took in the view.

'I can't see anything,' called Amorphous to Titty. 'I think it's the sunglasses.'

Titty craned her neck forwards. 'OK. Just hold it steady. You've got a lorry coming up on your left. OK, veer very slightly right. Stop, stop, stop! That's enough.'

By the time they reached Fort William Titty was beginning to get a cramp in her thighs and neck. 'I can't go on much longer,' she said. 'I've had my arse propped up here for 250 miles. The parcel shelf is chafing on my cheeks a bit.'

'Not long now,' replied Amorphous as he sped through the tourist town.

'Left, left, left, slow down, right a bit, a bit more,' instructed Titty. 'Could we at least get something to eat?' she begged. 'Left, left, left.'

Amorphous pulled off to the left and sped into McDonald's car park.

'Right, right, right, slow, slow right down,' said Titty. The Agent Provocateurs followed; but the youths in the double-decker had to hang back as they couldn't get under the height restriction barrier. Titty pressed her arse even harder against the window as the car slowed down and stopped at the drive-through intercom.

'Can A'help ya?' crackled a voice through the intercom.

'The question is not, can you help me? The question is, when are you going to help me?' said Amorphous.

'I'll help you now, sir. Can I take your order, please.'

Amorphous read the menu. 'I believe we shall have three half-pounders with cheese.'

'No!' boomed the Cheese Maker from the back. 'I'll make the cheese. It'll cost 75p extra if we all have their cheese.' He whipped out his tongue cleaner and ripped his pants down, grabbing hold of Monty.

Titty glared at him in a very strange way as he got to work right next to her. 'I'll have their cheese, to be honest, Amorphous, on mine,' she said. 'I think this guy's cheese might be a little mature and detract from the flavour of the burger.'

Amorphous placed the order, sped along to window three, paid and sped off, giving them a three-minute lead over the Agent Provocateurs, who couldn't decide what to have.

The bus was still on to them though. The boys seemed to be taking it in turns. One would drive and watch Titty's fantastic arse, while the other would be doing something on the upper deck. Three or four minutes later they'd swap over again. This went on for another 72 miles, all the way to Kyle of Lochalsh.

Titty was now flagging. Her arse had gone into spasm. She had terrible pins and needles in her thighs, and her back was aching from propping her arse up against the rear window. 'I can't take it any more,' she said, and collapsed forward.

Amorphous immediately smashed the car into a lamp-post. 'Aaagggggghhh!' shrieked the Cheese Maker as the tongue-cleaning wire wrapped around Monty, slicing him in half as the Cheese Maker's body was thrown forward into the front seat; Monty's top half flew out of the window and was crushed beneath the wheels of the bus.

'What's going on?' called Amorphous, collapsed in a heap in the driver's foot well. There was then another almighty smash as the bus piled into the back of the car, crushing it to half its size. Both the spotty youths were ejected through the window and impaled on the horns of a huge red stag who'd stopped to watch the action.

There was a stunned silence as the occupants of the Astra checked they were still alive.

'Amorphous?' said Titty.

'Titty,' said Amorphous. 'Cheese Maker?'

'Amorphous,' replied the Cheese Maker.

'Monty?' asked Amorphous.

The Cheese Maker began to blub and groan. He pulled himself out of the gap behind the seats and slumped into the crushed rear seats, clasping his bleeding stump. 'Monty's gone,' he cried. 'He's gone.' He looked out of the window and could just make out the little guy, a shadow of his former self, 1mm thick and over 12 inches wide, with dirty great bus tyre treads along his length. 'Goooonnnneee!'

The Agent Provocateurs had now caught up with

them. They sped round the corner through Kyle and were only stopped from smashing into the back of the Astra by the traffic lights which had turned red to let a group of American tourists cross. Titty grabbed the wheel of the Astra and reversed it as far back into the bus as it would go. She then swung the steering wheel round on full lock and squeezed the car out. It coughed and spluttered and scraped, but it moved. She pulled out into the main road, but the Astra immediately broke down.

'Get him out of here!' shouted Amorphous to Titty.

They all jumped out of the car. Titty grabbed the blubbing Cheese Maker. 'Put your stump back in!' she shouted, grabbed him by the arm and ran across the road to an old Massey Ferguson tractor which was parked outside the post office. 'Rank, get me instructions to hotwire a 450 Massey Ferguson,' she said down her phone.

Rank tapped furiously at his keyboard. Titty climbed into the driver's seat and hoisted the Cheese Maker in behind her. 'I've got hotwire directions for

International, John Deere and Lister … nothing for Massey Ferguson, though,' said Rank.

Just then a farmer walked out of the post office clutching the milk he'd bought for his dying sheepdog Bessie. 'Oooggg, man, yon's mi tractor!' he said politely to Titty.

Titty pulled her gun out from beneath her blue tit feather and shot him in the guts. She jumped down from the tractor, grabbed his keys and fired the Massey up.

Amorphous meanwhile was standing in front of the Hyundai brandishing his Swiss Army knife. The lights turned green, and Beacham stepped on it. The car roared towards Amorphous at a very moderate pace. Amorphous tried to leap out the way as it reached him, planning to slash the side with his penknife, but he misjudged and the Hyundai threw him backwards through the air.

'Amorphous!' cried Titty as he flew over her head. But he was safe. He landed on the roof of a 'Barry's of Virginia Water' tour bus that was transporting thirty or so octogenarians around the West Coast of

Scotland, so that they could get out for the toilet every nine or ten hours and marvel at the scenery. Titty pulled out behind the bus and the two vehicles headed towards the Skye bridge. The Hyundai was right behind them. The bus passed right through the bridge control with no problem, as Amorphous hung on to the roof. Titty, however, was asked for £5.40 to cross the bridge. 'Are you taking the piss?' she asked the daft twat behind in the control booth. '£5.40? It's only about 10 foot long!' she protested.

But the Hyundai was closing in. 'Sorry, madam. That's the toll.'

Titty turned her pistol on the man and shot him repeatedly in the chest and twice in the face. He fell to the ground to the screams of his colleagues. 'Well, it's ridiculous,' said Titty. 'It should be free.' She tore off at three miles an hour, leaving the poor staff to clean up their colleague's brains.

They hadn't got half way across the bridge when the Hyundai drew up alongside them. 'Down!' shouted Titty to the Cheese Maker. Cline emerged from the window, firing his machine gun. Incredibly, none of the hundreds of bullets he fired the five feet over to the tractor hit either Titty or the Cheese Maker. Titty swung the tractor across the road and started heading down it the wrong way. A car travelling towards her at over sixteen miles an hour was forced to swerve violently and nearly drove straight off the bridge.

This formation of the tractor under close-range heavy machine-gun fire continued for eight miles, all the way to the village of Broadford. Then an amazing thing happened. Realizing that they had left a mad old duffer wandering around the loos at Kyle of Lochalsh, the 'Barry's of Virginia Water' tour bus turned round and went back.

Amorphous was waiting for his chance. He braced himself as the tractor and Hyundai came into view, driving straight at the coach. He could just make out the barrage of heavy gunfire and was amazed that not one of the bullets had travelled the three feet from the gun to Titty or the Cheese Maker on the cabless tractor. As the coach drew closer the Hyndai and tractor separated. The Hyundai went down the right-hand side of the coach and the tractor the left. Amorphous turned onto his stomach and reached over to hoist the Cheese Maker off the tractor.

'Over here!' shouted Titty, seeing that Amorphous still had his sunglasses on. Amorphous flailed about, grabbing frantically with his arms. Titty just managed to shove the Cheese Maker into his grasp as the tractor chugged past.

The Agent Provocateurs were surprised when they swerved back round the end of the coach into Titty. The Cheese Maker was gone. They stayed next to the tractor for another mile or so, firing constantly, before realizing she was no good to them and letting her go. Cline then morphed himself into Barry of 'Barry's of Virginia Water' and took control of the bus. He rocketed across the Kyle Straits, hung a swift left at the roundabout and over the bridge. Amorphous and the Cheese Maker hung onto each other; trying desperately to keep their grip on the roof of the coach as it swung this way and that.

Suddenly Beacham appeared on the roof armed with a balsa wood aeroplane. 'Hello, Mr

Amorphous. I bet you think you're pretty smart, huh? Think you can outsmart this?' He held up the aeroplane, grinned and ran at Amorphous, smashing the plane across his head. The flimsy toy splintered and broke over the large man's temple.

Amorphous grabbed Beacham in a mud-wrestling bear hug and squeezed hard. 'Take that, you big ruffian!' he yelled.

Beacham coughed and gasped as the air was forced out of him. But he managed to get a hand free and chopped Amorphous in the neck. 'Blam!'

Amorphous stumbled backwards, losing his grip on the coach roof. He wrenched his penknife out of his pocket and stuck it through the metal roof, just in time to save himself as his body fell off the back of the coach. He granced up at the knife, which was looking precarious, and then below him at the road and Kyle Sound.

Beacham appeared over the edge, grinning at him. 'I believe, Mr Amorphous, that your time may have come.' He held his gun out and fired repeatedly into Amorphous's head at point blank range. Amazingly, none of the bullets hit, and Amorphous managed to swing himself up into the air and back-flip onto the roof of the coach. Beacham swung round to face him, but Amorphous was too fast and planted a boot right in his face. Beacham went flying backwards off the coach, landing with an almighty thud onto the bonnet of a Skoda Felicia. He rolled over and looked through the smashed windscreen; there cursing at him was Nairobi.

'Goddamn motherfucker, hoochie ass bitch, low down hoe bitch mutherfucker!' she swore.

Steak Fork leaned over from the back seat and shot Beacham in the head twice. It was too late, though. Beacham was gone.

'Hold on tight!' shouted Amorphous as the coach rounded the corner of the bridge.

'The toll,' called the Cheese Maker to Amorphous.

Amorphous span round to try and see, but he couldn't really.

Suddenly the coach screeched and jerked violently as Cline hit the brakes. 'I didn't know you had to pay both ways,' he growled as the coach jack-knifed across the road, throwing Amorphous and the Cheese Maker into the air and flattening the toll booth where Beacham was waiting to take the fare. 'You don't pay both ways on the Severn Bridge,' continued Cline as the coach smashed to a halt, just before it exploded into flames, killing many of the innocent wrinkly old tourists.

Amorphous and the Cheese Maker landed on Newo, who was just getting off the train from Inverness. His body took the enormous impact of the two large men, which threw him backwards into the buffet car. Luckily the impact was cushioned by Vanessa Feltch, who just happened to be buying herself eight BR burgers for breakfast.

CHAPTER TEN

THE GEEKS ARE REVOLTING

And so it fell to those with the knowledge to destroy the Matewix. They had spoken to the Mog and they had the Cheese Maker, although no one was really sure what to do with him. Amorphous gathered them all together in a dark room where some wore sunglasses to look cool, while others wore leather and other tight-fitting fabrics; except the Number Two, who knew nothing but Laura Ashley.

'Together we stand today, friends,' Amorphous addressed the others, 'we who have fought so long … we who have fought for *freedom*!' Amorphous threw his hands in the air and swung round in triumph to the audience of Titty, Newo, Nairobi, Phil Offeastenders and the Cheese Maker. 'Freedom, my friends, freedom from the constraints of *robots*!' He did the arms in the air thing again. The others viewed him quizzically. 'The freedom to do what *we* want. The freedom to drive at thirty miles an hour in a built-up area and seventy on the freeway – the freeway! My friends, we have fought for the freedom to eat at McDonald's and listen to Britney Spears! The freedom to slave away at our computers for fifty hours a week so that we *can* spend the weekend chasing ducks round a nuclear cooling lake on a caravan toilet, before going off to the mall with the kids to buy stuff! It is this freedom, the freedom to spend the first sixteen years of our lives in a cruel and strict institution learning about the wives of Henry the Eighth and Long Shore Drift, that makes us human. Human, my friends – biologically superior to any other creature on this earth.'

'What about –' interrupted Phil Offeastenders '– what about leopards?'

Amorphous smiled and shook his head. 'We make leopards look like twats, Phil Offeastenders.'

'What ab'at pussy motherfuckers?' asked Nairobi.

Amorphous shook his head again. 'All of the felids – we make them all look like idiots. You ever see a human using a litter tray or catching rats in their mouths?' explained the great man.

'Shrews?' ventured Titty. 'What about shrews? They are the only mammal with poisonous teeth.'

Amorphous shook his head once more. 'Again, my darling Tit, shrews just don't cut it in the real world. You ever seen a human being eaten by an owl?'

Newo stepped forward. 'Waccoons? What about Waccoons?' he asked.

'That's just racist,' replied Amorphous.

Amorphous went through a huge chunk of the world's fauna and a small percentage of the flora, explaining in detail how each creature was in some way inferior to the human race. He got stumped for a bit on sea horses: the whole males giving birth thing seemed to be a source of enormous envy to him. But he eventually dismissed them on the basis that 'You try running the National on a fucking sea horse!' This discourse eventually came to a conclusion when all, including Amorphous, had fallen fast asleep.

Later, when they awoke, Amorphous briefly covered the marsupials, before concerning himself and the others with the more pressing matter of destroying the Matewix and offering them all some Dairy Lea on toast.

'The Matewix is a very complex screensaver,' he explained. 'To our knowledge it was created by a very clever bloke called Archie Text. He originally created the Matewix to protect people's computer monitors from being ruined when not being used for long periods of time. But his creation spiralled out of control, affecting almost all of the world's computers and rendering them useless. That is why, my friends, we use ZX81s: they are so useless that installing the Matewix screensaver on them would require over 200 ZX81s wired in sequence, just to see a static picture on the monitor! So it has fallen quite painfully into our laps to destroy the Matewix.'

'What about the Mainfwame?' asked Newo.

'Yes, Newo, the Mainfwame. That is why we have the Cheese Maker,' explained Amorphous. 'He may be a complete arsehead' – the Cheese Maker locked slightly put out – 'but he has the knowledge ... Take it away, Cheesy!'

The Cheese Maker sat forward, a little embarrassed. 'I used to make cheese for an individual in Weston-Super-Mare,' he began. 'He was a strange man, grey of hair, yet somehow obsessed, even at his age, with lashings of Dairy Lea on hot white toast.' The others screwed their faces up in disgust. 'He was, however, an agoraphobe and was thus incapable of walking the two or so hundred yards down onto the Locking Road Spar to buy himself any of the chemical-exploration-based product. He thus charged me with the job of producing and delivering to him the product on a daily basis. At first I was of the opinion that the creation of Dairy Lea was impossible without a large factory and a huge quantity of chemicals; but I discovered one day, while fiddling with my cock on the loo, that I had the unique ability of being able to create it myself. I thus started jarring it, using a spoon at first, then a cheese wire, but later moving on to the tongue-scraper that I use now. I can produce about a kilo a day if I don't wash and am thus a walking cheese factory.'

The Cheese Maker looked very pleased with himself. The others looked a little horrified, and some put down their Dairy Lea on toast.

'To the point, please, Mr Cheese,' said Amorphous.

'Oh yes, the point,' resumed the Cheese Maker. 'This man, who I knew as Archie Text, spent almost every daylight hour working on something on his computer. From what I can remember it appeared to be just pages and pages of jumbled green writing. Granted he was profoundly dyslexic; but he assured me that he was creating a story in which machines ruled the world and humans were their slaves.'

Newo looked sceptical. 'He was just a witing a novel, then?'

The Cheese Maker thought for a moment. 'I suppose it is possible, yes … but there's another thing.' The group sat forward to hear what it was. 'He had pictures of … you all over his walls!' He pointed at Newo.

Newo sat back, horrified. 'Of me?' he shrieked, pointing at himself.

'Well, it looked like you. It was about twenty-five years ago and you were a lot younger then.'

'I was five then,' replied Newo.

'Well, it was quite a likeness,' insisted the Cheese Maker. 'Same nose.'

Newo looked sceptical again.

'The Mainfwame is thus to be found in the home of the Archie Text,' explained Amorphous. 'Our job is to … destroy that building.'

'It will not be easy, though,' explained the Cheese Maker. 'He's got a burglar alarm.'

Amorphous shook his head. 'He has more than a burglar alarm now. He has a burglar alarm with motion sensors and Red Care® CCTV in his back garden, a Springer Spaniel and, perhaps worst of all, Neighbourhood Watch!'

The group looked disturbed. 'We'll have to disable his alarm,' said Titty.

'We'll have to shut down the electricity for the whole area!' said Phil Offeastenders.

'Goddam motherfuckers. Naawhaamsayin?' said Nairobi. 'Sands lak a Thir' Worl' booty call ta me!'

'We will need to destroy the whole of Weston-Super-Mare,' Amorphous told them. 'This will not be easy. Thousands of miserable scowling old blue rinses will be vaporized in their beds, unable to write to the BBC complaining about ITV dramas any more. The pier with its amusement arcade and stalls selling hot dogs and candyfloss to people who have only just crawled out of the sea will be destroyed, and the likes of Jethro and Jim Davidson will go out of business as a result. If you don't want that blood on your hands, then leave now.' Nobody budged an inch.

'Well then, we are agreed,' said Amorphous. 'First we must plant an enormous bomb on the sea front. Then we must tell the entire town that free tea and bingo will be served above the bomb that evening, thus gathering them all together in one place. The Archie Text is an agoraphobe and thus will be the only person, bar the infirm, who will not be seduced by the lure of free tea and bingo. Titty will detonate the bomb by placing her two incredible thighs on the detonator plunger thing and forcing it down with her buttocks. Most of Weston will then be destroyed.

Nairobi and Phil Offeastenders, you will take out the Congresbury phone exchange at exactly the same time with another big bomb, thus rendering the Red Care® remote response alarm system useless. When all this has happened, I will shoot the Springer Spaniel several times in the head, thigh and gut. Then Newo, the Cheese Maker and me will go in –'

'That's "I",' corrected Phil Offeastenders.

'What's "I"?' demanded Amorphous angrily.

'That's "Newo, the Cheese Maker and I", not "Newo, the Cheese Maker and me". You don't say, "I is going in," do you?'

Amorphous shook his head. 'You are not going in,' he replied, 'so shut up.' He recovered his composure. 'Are you getting all this, Rank?' he asked down the phone.

'Loud and clear,' replied Rank from the *Knobachaneza*.

'Stake Fork?'

'10–4,' replied Splattatechi from the Mr Whippy.

'There is a three-minute gap between *Countdown*

finishing and the Archie Text taking his afternoon nap. We will do it then.'

Later the crew were back on the *Knobachaneza*. Titty and Newo were taking afternoon tea and discussing their favourite television programmes.

'Oh, I weally like that Ainsley Hawwiot; he's so funny the way he pwetends he's clumsy all the time and the way he camps it up pwetending to be a bender. That kills me!'

Titty smiled. 'I think he's a complete cock,' she replied. 'I'm more of a Delia girl myself.'

'Oh. What about Gawwy Whodes? He's a cwazy guy; his false enthusiasm and painfully simpewing smile are fantastic. And that haircut … it weally puts him a cut above the west! Get it! He is the Nigel Kennedy of cooking.'

Titty smiled. 'I think he's a cock as well.'

'Oh Titty, my sweet Titty,' cooed Newo, coming on all affectionate. 'I had a dweam, Titty. Not the one where I plucked your blue tit feather off like a spawwow hawk; nor the one whewe I bwought you off with my Michael Winnit commemowative Death Wish Five Charles Bwonson back massager; no. It was one where your buttocks were so tight that they got stuck to the detonator plunger and you were a sitting duck, incapable of escaping the Agent Pwovocoteurs as they first poured honey over you, then covered you in locusts. Don't go into the Matewix, Titty, not tonight. Pleeeaaaassseeee. Pretty please.' Newo fell to the floor clutching Titty's hand.

She looked down, wondering what she had ever seen in him. So soppy, so wet. 'Newo, can you get up, you're making my dress filthy down there,' she said as sympathetically as she could. 'Listen, Newo, you're quite cute and everything, and, yes, that time you brought me off with your nose in that chimney stack in Slough was, well, pleasurable. But to be honest … I've been shagging Phil Offeastenders.'

Newo looked horrified and fell back in a particularly camp manner. Titty picked up a scatter cushion and fiddled with the frill. 'Phil Offeastenders!' cried Newo. 'Why? Why him?' he begged.

'I don't know, he just used to come into my room at night,' replied Titty in the most sympathetic way she could deliver such killing lines.

'But he's wed!' said Newo.

'Wed?' exclaimed Titty, getting to her feet. 'Cheeky bastard never told me that! I'll kill him.' She slid open the window of the *Knobber*, leaned out and fired three shots through the serving window of the Mr Whippy. There was a shriek and a scream and then a brief silence.

'Motherfucker. Naawhaamsayin!' shouted Nairobi. 'Wha goddam hoochie hoe motherfucker put a cap in da ass of da Eastender motherfucker?'

Titty realized what she'd done and ducked back in before anyone saw her. She sat back down next to Newo.

'I didn't mean mawwied,' explained Newo. 'I meant he's wed, his face is bwight wed, he looks like a beetwoot.'

Titty looked a little horrified. 'Not married, then?'

'No,' replied Newo.

'Just dead?'

256

'Yes, Titty.' Newo got up from the floor and sat down among the scatter cushions.

'Well, I've shagged Rank a few times as well,' Titty continued.

Newo fell backwards onto the floor again. 'What? Wank?'

Titty nodded.

'What in your wight mind were you doing with Wank?'

'I don't know,' replied Titty.

'I suppose *he* just used to come into your woom at night too, did he?' groaned Newo, burying his head in his hands. 'He'd just come at your whim, would he?' Newo began to cry.

'Don't cry, Newo,' said Titty, putting a hand on his back. 'The Mog told me that I would fall in love with the Number Two. So I'm sure I will at some point. But you can't force these things, can you?'

'The Mog, the Pwophet, the Owacle – what do any of them know?' cried Newo.

'You just need to be ... well, a bit more ... you know ... manly,' explained Titty as gently as she could. 'You know, the Laura Ashley dress, the slightly camp demeanour, the inability to pronounce your *r*'s, the Morris dancing and naked mud wrestling with Amorphous – it's all a bit, well ... bent, if you ask me.'

Newo stood up in his dress. 'Look,' he said. 'Look! I've got a fucking great horn, you dozy bitch! Does that look bent to you?'

Titty nodded. 'Well, in the dress ... yes.'

Newo shook his head. 'Well, I'm going to wig the pier with hundweds of pounds of twinitwotoluene and vawious other plastic explosives,' he hissed and stormed off, catching his cock on the door to the shower on the way.

'Free tea and bingo!!!!' came the voice from the loud hailer of the Mr Whippy. 'Free tea and bingo tonight!!!!' The Mr Whippy turned right along the sea front. 'Free tea and bingo on the pier tonight. And none of that new bingo lingo, either. It's the old stuff with legs eleven and the two fat ladies.' It appeared, from the faces of the residents and tourists in the beleaguered Somerset town, that this was a truly fantastic idea.

Nairobi took the mike and had a go. 'Goddam free tea, motherfuckers! Free tea and hoochie ass turkey bingo, motherfuckers!' she shouted.

Steak Fork snatched the mike back from her. 'Less of the swearing, boss,' he advised. 'These are traditional folk. They still blame swearing for the failings of their children, rather than themselves.'

'Motherfuckers!' Remarked Nairobi as she unwrapped a Twister and ate it whole.

The *Knobachaneza* was doing much the same as the Mr Whippy, except Rank was having to drive around the suburbs and do all the loud hailing because Newo and Titty weren't talking to each other, the Cheese Maker was an arsehead and Amorphous was useless on the mike because he kept deviating from bingo to Plato and banging on about the Matewix. By teatime the whole of Weston-Super-Mud was packed and heaving with wrinklys.

'Don't go!' begged Newo as the *Knobachaneza*

pulled up at the sea front. Newo and Titty had managed to spend the entire afternoon without uttering a single word to each other, despite Newo arriving back on the milk float wearing a flying jacket, jeans and rigger boots in a most manly style. But the sight of his beloved about to go to her death conquered his pride and he clung onto her arm like a lovesick koala. 'Plllleeeaaaasssssseee don't go.'

Amorphous and the Cheese Maker looked on, slightly disturbed by Newo's excessive wretchedness. Titty tried to wipe Newo off her arm but he was clutching it too tightly. 'Listen, Newo. As a superior officer on this milk float I order you to release me,' she tried.

Newo began to blub. 'You're not supewior to me,' he protested through his tears.

'I am, Newo,' she insisted. 'The order goes: Amorphous, me, Rank, you, the Cheese Maker.'

Newo shook his head. 'No, it doesn't ... blub, blub, blub ... I wank higher than Wank. I should wank over you and below Amowphous, but as it stands I wank between you and Wank ... with you wanking above me and me wanking over Wank. I understand that the Cheese Maker wanks awound the bottom, but weally we shouldn't be pulling wank. Being the Number Two I should wank over all of you anyway. I should be the highest wanking person in this woom!'

The others felt decidedly soggy by the time Newo had finished talking such wank. Titty grabbed his wrist and shoved him off. She jumped out of the door of the *Knobber*. 'Get a grip on yourself, Newo, before you turn into a total ranker!' she cursed, before running off with her detonator and cord to blow up the entire population of Weston. Here's an interesting fact: 50 per cent of the first 100,000 humans ever to walk the earth are still alive and resident in Weston-Super-Mare.

31 Chesham Road South was quiet and empty when Amorphous, Newo and the Cheese Maker arrived. The street had an eerie stillness to it, as if every elderly resident had somehow been annihilated by a genocidal temptress with incredible buttocks. Amorphous watched the street lights flicker and go

out. The lights in the houses all suddenly extinguished as well. 'Now, Titty!' he whispered down his phone.

Titty leaped into the air and came down on the detonator plunger with such a callipigeous force that the plunger not only fired a bolt of electricity down the fuse, blowing up the entire population of Weston, but also sent it right up her arse, where it got stuck, rendering her completely disabled. Two seconds later Amorphous, Newo and the Cheese Maker heard an almighty rumble as the bomb blast passed over them.

'Now!' ordered Amorphous.

The three men walked up to the house and rang the doorbell. Newo was back in Titty's dress, and Amorphous was in his Speedos. A dog barked furiously inside, but no one answered. Amorphous lifted his foot and kicked the door in. The door bolted straight out of its frame and shattered the occasional table just inside the door. A Springer Spaniel growled from the hallway, then ran at them playfully, wagging its tail.

'Hello, little boy,' said the Cheese Maker, bending down to greet it.

'Goodbye, bitch,' said Amorphous as he blew the creature backwards down the hall, firing at it repeatedly until it looked more like a King Charles Spaniel.

'That was a bit uncalled for,' complained the Cheese Maker angrily. 'He was only trying to play with us.'

Amorphous sneered at the Cheese Maker. 'He was an Agent Provocateur. I had no choice!'

The three men walked into the hallway, stepping over the corpse of the dog, and made their way up the stairs. At the top was a small, dimly lit green landing. Smiff was standing at the end of it, smiling.

'Hmmm ... Hello, Mr Amorphous, Mr Sanderson, Mr Wensleydale ... hmmm ... You just can't keep away, can you? Hmmm ...'

Newo stepped forward. 'What do you want, Smiff?' he asked.

Smiff grinned and looked at Newo's erection beneath the dress. 'Still using all the muscles except the important one, Mr Sanderson ... hmm.'

Amorphous stepped up. 'What do you want, Smiff?' he asked.

Smiff shrugged. 'Revenge, Mr Amorphous, revenge. I was ... er ... booted out of the program because of you ... And now I'm not allowed back in ... That hurts, Mr Amorphous, that really hurts. You ... killed me and then you ... killed me again. But I did not go away. I will not go away. As ... Socrates said, "I am not going to alter my conduct, not even if I have to die a hundred deaths."'

Amorphous whipped out his gun and fired straight at Smiff's head, which swerved round the bullet and returned to its normal position. Smiff grinned. 'And the beauty of me, my friends, is that there is always a good supply of me!'

Suddenly through doors on the landing and the hall poured more Smiffs, all staggering and all accompanied by fiendish embryos with tinny voices shouting directions. 'Left a bit, right a bit, forward!'

Newo shook his head. 'Not had time to sort out

the little guys, then?' he asked with a grin, then burst into action.

Smiff went flying backwards as Newo span and kicked him twice in a double Kent trot, a move devised by the earliest Morris dancers. He smashed into the wall. Newo glided round behind him and skipped up to two more Smiffs, kicking their embryos off along the way, leaving the Smiffs blind, before snapping both their necks with a twisting salco. These two fell on two others, knocking them to the ground in a pile of death and blindness. Amorphous was doing well, battering ten types of shit out of several more totally sightless Smiffs. The embryos were helping their hosts a little with directions and occasional gunfire from their tiny pistols, but the Cheese Maker was going round making short work of them, plugging their mouths with cheese, leaving them unable to communicate with their hosts and thus sitting ducks for the powerful Amorphous. Smiff got back up, though, drew his gun and started blazing. The Cheese Maker ducked below a couple of stiff Smiffs and hid. Amorphous took a shot in the arm and went down. Newo was forced to run up the wall, across the ceiling, from where he ripped Smiff's head clean off.

Suddenly there was silence, bar the odd wretched embryo spitting and cursing on the odd thigh. The Cheese Maker stood up. 'That's his room there,' he said to Newo.

Newo turned and looked down the corridor. There was a door at the end of it.

'You must go, Newo. You must open the door,' said Amorphous. Suddenly Smiff burst out of the toilet, all guns blazing. Amorphous span round to meet him. 'Go!' he shouted. Newo ran for the door and burst through it.

It was quiet inside. The room was dimly lit and smelled of stale milk. On the walls hung ragged, stained pictures of Pariah Carey with her saggy tits. There was a squat single bed in the corner of the room, with what appeared to be the lump of a human in it.

'Hello,' said Newo. 'Awe you Archie?' The body grunted. 'Archie Text?' The body moved a little and grunted again. 'My name is Newo.'

The sheets moved apart slowly and a small, gaunt man appeared. He looked very much like Wayne Sleep, lucky man, Wayne Sleep in his sixties with a Parker jacket. He peeked out, eyeing Newo suspiciously. 'What do you want with me?' he hissed.

'I have come to destwoy the Mainfwame,' explained Newo. 'I believe it is here.'

Archie removed the covers a bit more and sat up a fraction. 'Your person … matches almost every supposition I had considered preluding your arrival,' he said, sitting up a bit more. 'Conceivably I never considered a transsexual overtone underpinning any level of my genealogy.' He eyed the dress. Newo struggled hard to understand just what the hell he was saying. 'Do you find me attractive, Newo?'

Newo shook his head. 'Good God, no!' he protested.

'Apropos, my supposition concerns the almost perpendicular angle of your systemic anomaly.' Newo stared down at his cock. 'Pure persiflage, of course,' continued Archie, chuckling a little and clambering out of his bed.

'Do you know who I am?' asked Newo.

'Of course,' replied Archie. 'You have many questions. You are by your very nature … human … thus you are programmed by virtue of design with a certain inquisition that compels you to investigate trivialities beyond the necessity of their relevance. This peculiarity is obviously compounded in those with an extra X-chromosome; it is, however, inherent in all but an elite and is thus considered perhaps the norm. Concordantly, while you concern yourself with my appreciation of your existence, I wonder whether the conception of your conception has considered itself, at any point in your life, a concern to you as profound as which one of Girls Aloud you'd rather shag? I think not.'

Archie walked across the room and sat down next to his computer. Newo sort of smiled and tried to figure out the last paragraph. 'Of course, if you had entertained the dimorphism of which your existence was the eventual corollary, you would have perhaps attempted to draw conclusions. But due to the inherent banality of your being you failed to suppose anything but your introspective egregious concerns. Ergo, you have no idea who your parents are.' Newo thought for a moment and nodded.

Archie sat back in his chair and shook his head. 'I suppose didacticism is essentially unavoidable at this juncture, as your comprehension of patently simple concerns has hitherto failed to … keep up!'

Newo smiled and nodded. 'Yes,' he said. 'Twice!'

Archie smiled and nodded. 'The concatenation of your ancestry is complex in the extreme. I am perhaps more au fait with the conspiracy of your paternal lineages but feel that any explanation at this juncture would be perhaps too perfunctory. Suffice to say … I am your father!'

'What!' cried Newo. 'My father?'

Archie nodded. 'Indeed. You were the eventuality of a unbound conation of two perverse antecedents, an elicit union vis-à-vis your mother and me.' Archie slid forward in his chair and passed Newo a dictionary. 'Perhaps this will catalyse your abecedarian aspirations,' he said with a smile.

'My mother's a dinner lady in Godalming,' protested Newo.

'Contrary to your understandings, your maternal host was in fact, and though in evolutionary terms comparable and perhaps more deserving of a quadropedal stature than a dinner lady, a member of the taxonomic genus *felis*. Ergo, your mother was a domestic cat … *felis cattus*.'

Newo looked horrified. 'A cat!' he cried.

Archie nodded calmly. 'A domestic cat.'

'You fucked a cat?' cried Newo in disbelief.

Archie continued to nod. 'I believe you knew her as … Mystic Mog.'

Newo laughed a little. 'I can't believe I'm heawing this. You should be locked up. You're a bloody perv!'

Archie smiled. 'Indeed, I was caught *in fragrante delicto* by the RSPCA and consequently incarcerated for a full penal term and briefly institutionalized due to the grotesqueries of my trespass. Your mother was, however, bound by certain contradictory biological systemic anomalies and was thus inseminated by some form of immaculate conception ... hence the subsequent intrauterine existence of – the Number Two.'

Newo frantically flicked through the dictionary, thumbing words out and reading them. 'Why don't I have whiskers, then? Ha!'

'You have nine lives, Newo,' said Archie with a patronizing smile. 'The fertilization process by which you were constructed contained a coincidentally substantial percentage of deoxyribose nucleic acid carrying blueprint information specifically concerned with my physiology. Hence your stature. Certain characteristics, however, idiosyncratic with felid behaviour remained inextricably within you; consequently you prefer to defecate on the carpet rather than in a toilet; you meow during orgasm; and you are particularly susceptible to toxoplasmosis. A basic cognition, however, inherent in all humans, has enabled you to overcome various predisposed feline traits. To complete your concerns of my recidivism, I now abstain from any form of licentious union. Thus my reclusive continuance.'

Newo dropped the dictionary. 'Is it possible you could perhaps use words of less than eighteen syllables, or perhaps talk slower so that I can keep up?'

The Archie Text swung round in his chair, chuckling to himself. 'You are in love, aren't you, Newo?' he asked paternally. Newo nodded. 'You are, however, and quite distressingly, considering the line of your descent … a virgin!'

'No, I'm bloody not!' protested Newo.

The Archie Text smiled wryly to himself. 'A cri de Coeur, my son? I consider the question of the order *aves* and the genus *hymenoptera* a simplistic diagram; perhaps too rudimentary at this juncture of your life. Let me concern this discourse with, perhaps, a more complex illustration of the nature of concupiscence and the resulting physical dimension that occurs as a result of such deliberation. The man, overcome by sexual euphoria, interfaces his condyloidal apode with the perianthical opening of the woman's construct. Assuming he has no painful condyloma on his isthmus, he is then free to conspire with his lustful aspirations pain-free for up to 180 seconds, until the union of his … condottiere and the female's magnanimous receptacle form a confluence; whereby an embryo is formed … Ergo, you just horse it in there, son!'

Newo nodded. He was becoming impatient. He kept thinking of Titty, what she'd said to him, what he'd said to her. It ran around in his brain and hurt him.

Archie picked up his remote control and flicked the television on. 'The feelings you sustain for this creature are purely erogenous and thus by their very nature mere shibboleth, of course.'

Titty was on the local news! She appeared to be stuck, sitting atop a detonator plunger, spinning round and firing repeatedly at the police, who had called in marksmen to shoot her. 'The boy in you wants to run to her … hmm … The Machiavellian wants to stay, though, which I surmise is indicative of your true emotion – lust, not love. Newo, the fervour with which you hold this … woman … is thus erroneous in the extreme. She will not be the one to

… execute your maidenhead – if a man had such a thing. I thus advise you to take a more bestial approach to your concupiscences.'

Newo felt rushed. 'Look here, cat burglar. Where's the Mainfwame? My job is to destwoy it and that's what I must do. If you stand in my way much longer I shall … wemove you.'

Archie smiled and crossed his legs. He placed his fingertips together in a praying position and smiled at Newo. 'Do you know what the Matewix is, Newo?' he asked.

Newo nodded. 'Yes sir, yes sir, I do.'

Archie smiled. 'No sir, no sir, you do not. You think you know what the Matewix is, but you do not. Let me explain.'

Newo shrugged and sighed. 'OK. Go on then.'

'Due to the inherent failings of more antediluvian ray tubes, I was charged, some time in the eighth decade of the twentieth century, to devise a program by which damage was not incurred by an excessive and sustained luminance reacting with the chemicals inherent in the make-up of the … computer monitor.

At first a simple photograph of a kitten would suffice. But trends forced a diversity and progression, leading in the second year of the Matewix to ... a picture of a mountain range in Yosemite National Park. This misprogression of essentially static illustrations continued for several years irrespective of my obligation – computer monitors were still sustaining irrevocable damage. I thus stumbled upon the fifth Matewix – a constantly streaming astral plain. It proved popular; everyone had one, their own computer-generated universe. However; bound by the pressures of technological innovation I was forced to ... evolve the screensaver. Which leads inexorably to you, Newo.'

Newo's eyes lit up at the sound of his name. 'Me?' he asked.

'Yes, Newo. You. You are, in your current manifestation, the result of a psychochemical delusion. Your comprehension of your environment is entirely individual, Newo. Individual to someone else. Indeed, a man who's psychosis is so profound that he has placed a cerebral umbrella over the minds of you and your … associates. I refer of course to Amorphous. Employed once crediting management executives with loyalty points for a major airline company, he became monotonized. Instead of maximizing his extroverted characteristic, he instead imploded introspectively, gravitating more towards the visual complications of the office computer than with the social niceties of other hominids. He began to try and read the Matewix, believing he was seeing scrolling pictures rather than scrolling words, some structures of which corroborated his astronomical delusion. This delusion promptly became intransigent and, with the intervention of various psycho-tomimetic substances, permanent. Amorphous thus became convinced of various subversive dictatorial conspiracies – robots taking over the world, etcetera … So acute was the reality of Amorphous's paranoid predicament that he was bound to create an autonomous role for himself and disseminate various concerns in the hope of recruiting warriors to fight the battle in his brain. Ergo, you are not actually the Number Two! You are Abednego!'

Newo's head began to shake uncontrollably as the millions of syllables bounced around in it. He clutched at various words as if talking to a Frenchman and, despite convincing himself he was nearly catching up, hadn't actually made it past the first sentence.

He turned to the television as the local news cut back to the Weston-Super-Mare sea front. Titty was still stuck by the virtues of her tight thighs to the detonator handle. She looked hot and exhausted. Sweat was dribbling down her neck onto her breasts and welling around her nipples, before overflowing down her silky-white stomach and slithering into her knickers.

'They're going to kill her!' shrieked Newo, as she span round firing an empty gun. 'She's out of ammo! I must go.' He turned for the door.

'It is too late, Newo,' said Archie. 'She is already dead. She was dead before you arrived here.' Newo looked horrified. 'This is not live television, Newo.' Newo looked at the screen just as Titty was shot twice in the heart by a police marksman.

'I can save her,' he pleaded.

'You can't, Newo. She is dead.' Newo went white and slumped into a chair. 'Titty is a dog,' said Archie.

'What!' exclaimed Newo, leaping to his feet. 'What did you say?' he shrieked aggressively.

'Titty is a dog, Newo. She is an eighteen-stone legal secretary from Leighton Buzzard.'

Newo shook his head. 'You're insane.'

Archie tried to look sympathetic. 'Titty is the manifestation of your own steaming desires, Newo. She is no more real than the Matewix. She is the result of a psychosexual apperception, brought on by various hallucinogens proffered to you by one Amorphous, or Ainsley Chariot as he is legally known.'

'But I've just watched her being shot by the police,' protested Newo.

Archie shook his head. 'No you didn't, Newo. What you saw was Sharon O'Tracy being shot by police … all eighteen stone of her.'

'No,' insisted Newo, shaking his head. 'It can't be.'

Archie nodded to confirm what he was saying.

'That is why she got stuck up the chimney in Slough. It was a cooling tower, Newo.'

Newo shook his head some more. 'No, no, I don't believe it.' His erection began to droop.

'When you were offered the blue pill, Newo, Amorphous was honest concerning its effects; it was essentially a very refined form of Viagra. However, he was less accurate on his portrayal of the effects of the red pill. What Mr Amorphous failed to mention to you was that it contained very high levels of lysergic acid, combined with a quantity of methylenedioxy-methamphetamine and traces of phencyclidine. You were, let us say for the sake of argument, absolutely tripping your tits off, Newo. Indeed, the last week of your life has been like a dream, Newo. Like Alice going down the rabbit burrow, only the rabbit in your case is pink.'

'No!' Newo continued to defy the truth.

'Yes, Newo. So overcome were you by the hal-lucinogens that you even acted out a psychodrama with your associates – a collective psychodrama to the extent that various suggestions by Amorphous manifested in a loose paradigm governing all associates. You, however, uniquely believed that you were somehow divine, that you were a warrior, that you had psychokinetic abilities. Hmmm. And while hundreds of innocent people died in your path, you continued to play out the psychodrama, assuming that it had a degree of inevitability to it; which I suppose it does.' Archie's expression became more sombre. 'An inevitability which exists in the real world, Newo. The world you don't believe in. The drugs will wear off. Your subsequent incarceration, however, will not.'

Newo shook his head and chuckled. 'I've had enough of this. I'm leaving,' he said.

Archie nodded. 'There are two doors here, Newo. The one on your left leads to Amorphous, the Cheese Maker, police custody and the brief continuation of your psychosis. The door on your right leads to the toilet and the porno wing I've had added onto the side of my house. It is up to you to decide.'

Newo moved closer to the door on his left. 'You'd

better hope we don't meet again,' he said as he grasped the door handle.

'Well, if we do, be sure to bring a dictionary,' said Archie with a grin.

Newo opened the door and left.

Amorphous leaped on him the second he was out the door. 'What did he say to you, Newo?'

Newo shook his head. 'Haven't got a clue … didn't get a word of it.' He shook his head some more. 'Mad as a bwush!'

Outside, the house was surrounded by police. Smoke rising from the burning pyre of octogenarians darkened the sky and stank of death. Police had shot and killed a mad, obese, genocidal woman in the centre of Weston and two more equally insane terrorists near the Congresbury telephone exchange. Their guns were now trained on the three final suspects a huge queen in a pair of red Speedos, a small wiry arsehead who scraped cheese off his cock with a tongue scraper and a goofy twat in a Laura Ashley dress who couldn't say his r's pwoperly: men or warriors, depending on how you look at them;

wanted for the murder of hundreds of policemen and innocent people, arson, illegal use of firearms, robbery, burglary, cruelty to animals, indecent exposure, Class A drug use and supply, counterfeit dairy production, several traffic offences, and Morris dancing.

'Get us out of here, Wank,' said Newo calmly down the phone. 'It's all been a complete waste of time.'